PUPPET

First published 2024 by Walker Books Ltd
87 Vauxhall Walk, London SE11 5HJ

2 4 6 8 10 9 7 5 3 1

Text © 2024 David Almond
Illustrations © 2024 Lizzy Stewart

The right of David Almond and Lizzy Stewart to be identified as author and illustrator respectively of this work has been asserted in accordance with the Copyright, Designs and Patents Act 1988

This book has been typeset in Gill Sans MT Pro

Printed and bound by CPI Group (UK) Ltd, Croydon CR0 4YY

British Library Cataloguing in Publication Data:
a catalogue record for this book is available from the British Library

ISBN 978-1-4063-9161-9

www.walker.co.uk

MIX
Paper | Supporting
responsible forestry
FSC® C171272

PUPPET

DAVID ALMOND

illustrated by Lizzy Stewart

WALKER
BOOKS

Also by David Almond

A Song for Ella Grey
Annie Lumsden, the Girl from the Sea
Bone Music
The Boy Who Climbed into the Moon
The Boy Who Swam with Piranhas
Brand New Boy
Clay
The Colour of the Sun
Counting Stars
The Dam
The Fire Eaters
Half a Creature from the Sea: A Life in Stories
Harry Miller's Run
Heaven Eyes
Kit's Wilderness
Mouse Bird Snake Wolf
My Dad's a Birdman
My Name Is Mina
The Savage
Skellig
Slog's Dad
The Tale of Angelino Brown
The Tightrope Walkers
The True Tale of the Monster Billy Dean
The Woman Who Turned Children into Birds

For Julia
D.A.

For Ivy
L.S.

one

1

Silvester woke from his dreams. He climbed the steep stairs to his attic. He hadn't been up here for years. An owl hooted somewhere near by. There was night-time traffic, not too far away. The moon shone brightly through the window to the sky.

Silvester was the puppet master who hadn't put on a puppet show for years, who thought he'd been forgotten by the world. But in the past few weeks, everything had begun to change.

There were posters on the walls from ancient times. Posters that told of performances by Silvester's Magical Puppet Theatre all around the globe.

He sat down at his workbench, brushed away some dust and cleared the cobwebs. He switched on the little lamp there, and sat for a while, his hands in its pool of light.

He seemed to be thinking hard, or maybe he was still dreaming.

On the workbench, bits of puppet lay in the dust. There was a box of half-made upper legs and lower legs, a box of half-made arms. Bits of wood that had turned into nothing yet. Dark wood, pale wood, heavy wood, light wood. Half-carved hands, a few misshapen feet. Lumpy torsos, skinny torsos. A few unfinished heads dangled on strings from the ceiling. There were old tubes of paint and pots of glue. Tweezers and needles and drills and bits of sandpaper and tiny saws. Curls of wire and lengths of string. A box full of clothes.

Just bits and pieces. Fragments.

Silvester sighed. How wonderful to be among these things again, to be in his attic again, to be at his bench again.

It was like coming to life again.

Spiders spun on strings in the moonlight and woodlice crawled over the bench. Down by the skirting board, a little mouse squeaked.

"Hello, spiders," said Silvester. "Hello, woodlice. Hello, little mouse." He let a spider run across his hand, and he smiled at the tiny tickling it made.

"Hello, owl," he said to the owl that hooted outside once more.

Somewhere a baby started to cry, and then was calmed again.

"Night-night," Silvester whispered. "Sweet dreams, little one."

He stared into the moonlight, then set to work.

He used thin wire and tweezers to put together a leg and then another leg. One was longer than the other; one had a very wobbly knee joint. One was dark wood; one was light. He added feet: one with a black boot, one with a brown. He found a pair of arms, one of them with powerful-looking muscles. One hand had the full four fingers, the other only three. He found a skinny torso and wired the arms and legs to it. He took one of the dangling heads from its string. It was pine wood, yellowy brown. He attached it to the body.

His hands moved swiftly.

"Be brave," he whispered to himself. "Be as good as you ever were."

He laughed at the puppet taking shape in his hands.

"What a funny-looking thing you are!" he said.

He sandpapered its cheeks then waxed them. He coloured its eyes green. He glued a few strands of black wool to the head for hair. Much tidier!

He stared into its eyes.

"Hello, Puppet," he said.

Inside him, memories were moving. He had made his first puppets long, long ago, when he was just a little boy, living

just a few streets away. He made them from clothes pegs and ribbons, from sticks and stones, from folded paper, from buttons and thread.

He used to give them names and make them move and he had conversations with them. He used to make up stories where the puppets flew to the moon or battled with dragons or travelled through time.

He used to take them to his mam and say, "Look at the thing I made, Mam!" He made them talk to her.

"Hello, madam," they said if they were being polite.

"Hello, you nitwit!" if they weren't.

Mam would join in. She'd pretend to be delighted or mortally offended. And she'd always say, "Silvester, what a clever lad you are!"

He smiled to imagine himself as a boy again, to hear her voice again.

"Was it really so long ago?" he whispered to himself.

He took a green shirt and a pair of brown trousers from the box of clothes, and he dressed the puppet. He put a little brown cap on its head.

He held the puppet up before him. It was as tall as a young child.

He held the puppet's arms out wide.

"I wonder," he said, "what strange kind of story you might be in?"

He moved the puppet back and forth across the bench.

He made it march; he made it leap; he made it fly.

He made it roar as if it was angry or wild.

He made it sing and giggle and laugh.

"A very serious story," he said in a very serious voice.

"A very silly story," he said in a very silly voice.

"Maybe a tale where you fall in love," he said, "or a tale filled with perilous adventures. Or maybe you'll fly to Mars, or get eaten by tigers, or…"

He laughed and laughed to himself.

How wonderful it was to be making a puppet.

He looked into the puppet's eyes again. "Hello, Puppet," he said.

And the puppet said, "E-O."

Silvester stared.

Puppet stared back at him with green eyes that were flat and empty.

Ah, it was just a dream. It had to be.

"Hello," Silvester said again.

No answer.

"Silly Silvester," he said to himself.

He laid the puppet in the dust and gently touched its cheek. He yawned. It was very late. Time to sleep.

"Night-night," he whispered. "See you in the morning."

He switched off the light and went back down the steep stairs.

Yes, he needed to sleep.

2

The past weeks had been rather busy, rather strange. It started with a letter from a museum. It seemed Silvester hadn't been forgotten after all. They wanted to make an exhibition of his work. His puppets, his costumes and his stages would be displayed for all the world to see. And of course Silvester said yes. He'd be so proud to have his work on show for evermore. So it was all arranged. And one morning when Silvester was in his kitchen having breakfast, there came a knock at the door.

Two men were standing there.

"Hello, Silvester," said one. "My name is Francis, and this is Sol. I think you're expecting us."

Silvester smiled and stepped aside and welcomed them in.

Francis and Sol had a load of boxes and bags and packing cases and labels. They hauled them inside.

"You're hard to find!" said Sol. "I didn't even know this lane existed."

Then he stood dead still and gasped in amazement.

"Goodness gracious me!" said Francis.

There it all was, spread around the living room, the remnants of Silvester's Magical Puppet Theatre. There were dozens of puppets, some of them as big as a child, some no bigger than a toddler's hand, some as small as a finger. They were lying on the sofa and sitting on the chairs. They hung on strings from the walls. There were kings and queens and witches and wizards and ghosts and demons and wide-eyed little girls and boys. Animals and dragons and monsters and fairies.

Scenery and costumes and curtains were laid out on the furniture and spread out across the carpet.

"A lifetime's work," Silvester said.

For a time, the men from the museum just looked at these things in wonder.

When they set to work, they were nervous, and Silvester saw that they were worried about how he was feeling.

"It's all right," he told them gently. "Do what you have to do."

The men relaxed, but they were careful and gentle with everything. They kept saying how beautiful it all was, how wonderfully well made.

"I saw you," said Sol. "I saw your show."

Silvester smiled. "You did?"

"Yes. When I was a boy. You came to our school in South Shields. It was..." He suddenly reached out and lifted a particular puppet and laughed out loud. "And *he* was in it!" he exclaimed. "It was a play about the dark, dark forest!"

"Aha!" said Silvester. "How wonderful! This is Jack, and that was one of his very best shows."

"It was *fantastic*! I remember him tiptoeing deeper and deeper into the dark!"

"And do you remember how he ended up?" asked Silvester.

Sol chewed his lips and closed his eyes and remembered.

"Yes! Oh heck, the wolf got him. The wolf got you, Jack! You were eaten up by the *wolf*!"

Silvester nodded. "That's right! But he came back out again, didn't he?"

"Yes," said Sol. "I was just a little boy – I was scared stiff! You came back out again, Jack, and I laughed my head off!" He held the puppet up before his eyes. "Hello again, Jack," he said. "Remember me?"

The puppet said nothing, of course.

"I really believed you got eaten up!" Sol said. "I *saw* it happen! The wolf got you, its jaws opened … and gulp! Down you went."

He mimed being the wolf. He mimed eating up Jack.

"How on earth did you *do* it?" he asked Silvester.

Silvester laughed and shrugged. "Years of practice."

"It was magic," Sol told him. "It was like the puppets were really *alive*!"

Silvester smiled again. "That's what everyone said. Magic.

20

But it was just hard work and clever tricks."

He touched Jack's wooden brow. "Everybody wanted it to be real, didn't they, Jack?" he said softly. "That's what made it easy to fool them."

"I guess that's right," said Sol. He started to wrap Jack in tissue paper. "Sorry, Jack," he whispered. "Got to be done."

"Goodbye, my friend," said Silvester. "Thanks for all the shivers and the laughs. See you in the museum."

Sol laid Jack in his box.

He carefully wrapped more puppets. He handled them tenderly, as if each one were alive.

"Goodbye, my friend," whispered Silvester to each and every one. "Thank you, old pal."

"No kids to pass it all on to?" asked Francis.

"Sorry?" said Silvester.

"You've got no children to take over the puppet theatre?"

"Ah, no." Silvester shook his head. "There was just me and my Belinda, and now she's gone." He pointed to a photograph on the wall. "There she is," he said.

And there she was, his wife, looking at them, smiling at them from years ago when she was young.

Francis and Sol stayed all day.

They put the puppets into their boxes.

They folded costumes and slipped them into bags.

They wrapped sheets of scenery in bubble-wrap.

They folded curtains and laid them into cases.

Everything was carefully labelled.

Much of it was worse for wear, faded, snapped, cracked.

Francis said there were experts at the museum who would clean and restore what they could. But Silvester also heard him whisper to Sol that some of it might just have to be chucked away.

When everything was packed up, they left Silvester on his own again.

They said they'd be back with their van later in the week.

3

Soon afterwards, there was another visitor, a young woman called Louisa. She was from the university and she was writing a little history of Silvester's Magical Puppet Theatre. It would be on sale in the museum when the exhibition opened.

She asked lots of questions about his shows and his travels. Which was his first show? Which was his best? How many places did he perform in? What were his craziest experiences?

Silvester answered many of the questions, but he struggled with some.

He checked in old notebooks and scrapbooks.

"There's so much to remember," he said. "Sometimes the exact places and dates slip from my mind."

Louisa patted his arm. "That's OK," she said. "Memory plays tricks, doesn't it?" She scribbled lots of notes. "There'll be info on Google, I expect."

"Did *you* ever see one of our shows?" Silvester asked her.

"Me?"

"Yes. Maybe when you were a little girl."

"Oh. I'm sorry. No." She scribbled more notes. "To be honest," she admitted, "my parents didn't really approve of puppets."

"Didn't *approve*?"

"No. They said they were rather silly things."

"Poor you," murmured Silvester. "Poor parents." He shook his head at the thought. "Did *you* think they were silly?" he asked.

She pondered. "I think I did, for a little while. Then I started to grow up, and I realized they were rather wonderful."

He smiled. "That's good," he softly said.

Then he told her about a journey he and Belinda took to the Scottish islands. How they performed for families on a beautiful beach while a pod of dolphins leaped and leaped through the sea close by.

4

It was so strange that week to have the boxes stashed in the living room, and to think of all those puppets tucked up inside.

Sometimes Silvester leaned down to them, as if he expected the puppets to be whispering together or crying out to be set free.

Sometimes he tapped on the lids.

"Everything OK in there?" he asked. "Everybody happy?"

Sometimes he was filled with doubts. Was he right to give so much away, to let the museum have everything? But he knew he was. He wouldn't be creating any more shows, not at his age. And it was good that people could see it all, even though there'd be no stories, even though the puppets would be so very still.

And he had his memories. He had all the scrapbooks that he'd filled over the years, crammed with cuttings and photographs. There were fan letters from people of all ages, from all around the world. Photographs and posters hung on the walls of every room in his house. They were pictures of his theatre, of his puppets, of himself and lovely Belinda, when they ran the very best puppet theatre in the whole wide world.

5

Sol and Francis came back with the van a few days later. There was hardly room for it in the narrow lane. They parked just outside the house.

Silvester wanted to help them but Sol said no.

"It'd be awful if you fell and hurt yourself," he said.

"Make yourself a cup of tea," suggested Francis. "Won't be long till everything's done."

Silvester wanted to stamp his feet and tell them that he wasn't a feeble old man, that he was still a little boy at heart, but he didn't. They were just being gentle and kind, after all.

The two men carried everything out through the front door and carefully loaded it into the van.

"Goodbye, my precious friends," Silvester whispered. "Thank you for everything." Then he nodded. "You can close the doors now, Sol," he said.

Sol slammed the doors and locked them.

They all shook hands. They said they'd see each other again at the museum.

Silvester watched the van creep out of the lane towards the square, until it turned a corner and couldn't be seen again.

A few tears slid down his face.

"Never mind," he said. "It's for the best."

Back inside, he stood in front of the photograph of Belinda on the wall. He gazed into her lovely smiling face, her lovely brown eyes.

"That's it, then," he told her. "Everything's gone." And he smiled back at her. "But the book is being written, the museum is waiting, and we'll be remembered for evermore."

He went into the kitchen and made a cup of tea and a Cheddar cheese and pickle sandwich, his favourite.

"It's a new life, Silvester," he said to himself.

The day passed by.

An owl hooted somewhere.

"So what will you do now?" Silvester wondered to himself.

He wasn't really sure.

What *should* a puppet master do when he's getting old and his puppets are all gone? He pondered. Nothing came to mind, except the images of puppets and the fragments of stories that always came to mind. Maybe they would never ever stop.

Sometimes he laughed as he walked through the empty rooms. Yes, so much had been taken away, but he felt weirdly free. He felt young again.

More days passed by. He cleaned and tidied the house. He slept so well, better than he had for years. Night after night of deep, deep sleep.

Then there came a moonlit night when he woke from his dreams, and the attic seemed to be calling him.

He hadn't been up there for ages.

He looked at the steep stairway.

And he climbed.

And he sat at his workbench and made the new puppet.

And the puppet said, "E-O."

And Silvester didn't believe it.

It must have been a dream, mustn't it?

So he came back down again to sleep.

And again he slept well.

And so another night passed by.

6

It was the laughter of children that woke Silvester. It seemed to come from far away. He'd slept such a long time. Already it was the middle of the morning.

He made a pot of tea in the kitchen. He ate toast and marmalade. Marmalade. So delicious. He licked his lips. He laughed.

"Good morning, my lovely," he said to Belinda on the wall.

He looked at the living room. So empty and strange.

A church bell started ringing. Then he remembered the puppet that he had made last night. He laughed again.

"Of course I made a new puppet," he said to himself. "Did I ever *really* think I'd stop?"

He climbed back up the steep stairs to the attic.

"Good morning, Puppet," he said.

Puppet lay on the workbench just as Silvester had left him. A little black spider crawled across his chest. A pigeon goggled in through the window to the sky.

Silvester sat at the bench. He let the spider crawl across the back of his hand then he held his hand to the wall and watched it crawl away towards the ceiling.

"Spider!" he murmured. "What a strange and lovely thing you are."

He lifted Puppet up. He stood him on the bench and looked into his eyes. He stretched Puppet's arms out wide.

"Maybe I should call you Jack and send you like him into the dark, dark forest," he said. "But no. You're not a Jack. You are just yourself. Puppet."

He made Puppet flex his muscles. He made him stamp

his feet as if he was ready to walk or to run. He made him raise his fists as if he was ready to fight off an attacker.

"What a quick and strong puppet you are!" Silvester exclaimed.

He glanced up at the window to the sky.

"And look who's come to see you!" he said. "Hello, pigeons! This is Puppet. And look, here are the dangling spiders. And there are the woodlice crawling. And do I see you, little mouse? There is such an audience for you, my Puppet."

He made Puppet skip and dance across the bench then made him bow. Then he carefully laid him down again.

"Now it's time to put some strings on you," he said.

He reached for a box full of lengths of wire and string. He held a piece of string between his hands to check its length.

"This one?" he said. "We could fasten this to your left leg."

He searched the boxes for the little screw-in fasteners to attach the strings.

Puppet moved.

His left leg moved, all by itself.

Silvester blinked. *"No!"* he whispered to himself.

He found one of the fasteners. He pressed it to Puppet's left knee and began to twist. The puppet flinched.

Surely not.

31

Silvester pressed again. Again the puppet flinched. No!

The spiders dangled closer, closer.

Silvester put the fastener down. He didn't dare look properly. He didn't dare think. Out of the corner of his eye, he saw Puppet's left leg move, ever so slightly.

"Don't be scared," Silvester whispered to himself. He could hardly breathe.

He held Puppet by the shoulders and lifted him up. Puppet helped. He shifted his feet. He *did*. Silvester could feel him rising from the bench.

He made Puppet stand straight. He looked into Puppet's bright green eyes.

"Maybe we won't need strings after all," he said softly.

Puppet looked right back at him.

"Shall we try to get you to stand?" Silvester said. "I'll hold you steady and then let you go. OK? Just keep your legs strong and straight and you'll be standing."

He held Puppet straight.

"Ready?" he asked. "Steady?"

Puppet said nothing.

Silvester let go. Puppet toppled to the bench.

"Whoops!" said Silvester. "Are you OK?"

He tried again.

"Imagine there are strings," he said. "Imagine that I'm holding you, even when I let go."

He held Puppet up, let go, and Puppet fell again. He did it again, and Puppet fell again. There were more spiders now, and more woodlice, and another pigeon, and another little mouse.

Silvester picked Puppet up. "They're all watching," he whispered. "We'll do it for them, shall we?"

He held him up.

"Now," he urged.

When Silvester let go, Puppet did stand for one second, then two, then he tottered, and he fell.

"Well done, little Puppet."

Silvester picked him up again. "You can do it!" he said.

He held him; he let go. Puppet didn't fall. There were at least five long seconds when Silvester stared very hard and willed Puppet to stay standing.

"You *did* it!" he cried.

He looked around the attic at the spiders, the woodlice, the pigeons, the mice, the dust, the air, the sky.

"He *did* it," he said.

Then he stood Puppet up again and let go, and Puppet stood on his own.

And Silvester whispered, "Hello, Puppet."

And Puppet answered, "E-O."

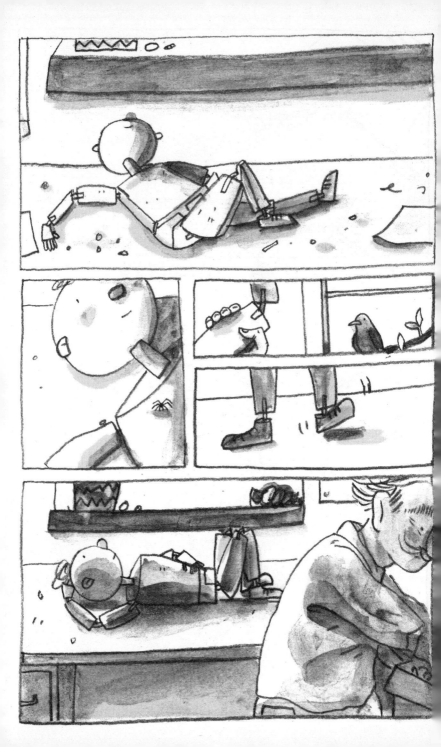

7

What a morning! Puppet learned so fast.

He stood all by himself several times before falling.

Pretty soon, Silvester said, "It's time you tried to learn to walk."

He lifted Puppet down from the bench and stood him on the floor. He held Puppet's shoulders and moved him gently forward, shifting him from side to side so that Puppet's legs swung forward one at a time.

"Get the idea?" said Silvester.

Puppet looked down at his feet.

"You move your feet one at a time," explained Silvester.

Puppet looked up at him.

"Watch me," said Silvester. "I'll demonstrate."

He sat Puppet on the edge of the bench, then he walked step by step across the room, swinging his legs and arms very slowly and deliberately.

"See?" He did it again. "Left, right," he said. "Left, right. One step then another. One step then another."

Sometimes he stumbled. He had to laugh at himself. It was weirdly hard to walk when he thought too much about it.

"Maybe I need strings myself!" he said.

But he kept on, and Puppet seemed to watch very carefully.

"Let's try again," said Silvester.

He lifted Puppet back down to the floor. He held Puppet's right shoulder with his left hand, reached down and lifted Puppet's right foot forward. He held Puppet's left shoulder with his right hand and lifted Puppet's left foot forward.

He let go, and *whoops*! Puppet fell.

They tried again.

Silvester held both Puppet's shoulders and eased him forward. He could feel it starting to happen. He could feel Puppet starting to move his legs and feet.

"Yes!" said Silvester. "Go on, Puppet. You can do it."

Puppet tried very hard.

"Imagine there are strings," said Silvester.

Puppet moved his left foot. He moved his right foot. Silvester took Puppet's hands and held them out above Puppet's head. Puppet swung his left foot forward; he swung his right foot forward.

"Shall I let go?" asked Silvester.

Puppet said nothing. He seemed to be concentrating.

"I will," said Silvester. "Ready?"

He let go, and *whoops*! Puppet tumbled to the floor.

They tried and tried, and Puppet kept on tumbling as the morning passed by.

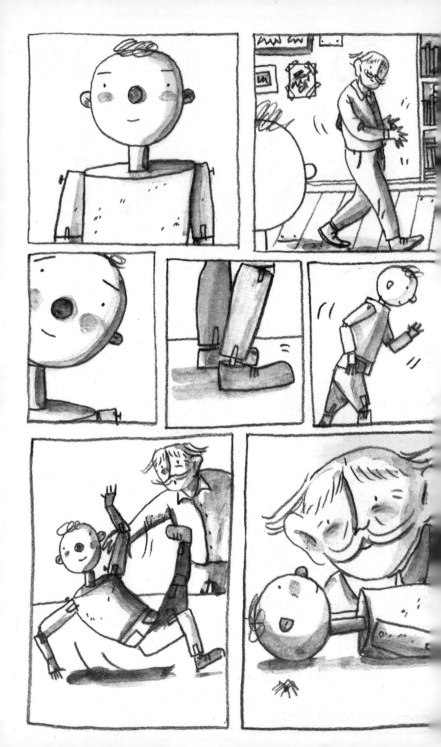

But at last there came the magic moment when Silvester held Puppet and then let go, and Puppet really did walk one step, two steps, three steps, four, before he fell.

And Silvester's heart stood still.

"Oh, my Puppet," he whispered. "You can *walk*!"

He looked at the spiders and woodlice and pigeons and the mouse down by the skirting board.

"Puppet can *walk*!" he said to them all.

Silvester lifted Puppet and sat him down on the edge of the workbench.

"My name is Silvester," he told him.

Puppet said nothing.

"And perhaps your name should be just Puppet. *Pupp-et.* Hello, Puppet."

Puppet gazed at Silvester for a long time, and then his mouth moved.

"E-O," he said.

Silvester laughed. Then he paused.

"Maybe one day," he said, "you might call me Dad. *D-ad*."

"E-O."

"Never mind. Maybe one day... But hello is enough for now."

"E-O."

"Hello, *hell-o*, my lovely boy!"

Silvester hugged Puppet and ran around the room with him. He called out, "Yes! I have a walking talking puppet!"

Resting his hand on the edge of the workbench, he stopped to catch his breath.

"Sorry. I got a bit carried away, Puppet. Time for a spot of lunch, I think. What would a puppet like for lunch? Who could ever know? Jam? Yes, maybe jam would be the best thing."

"Jam!" said Puppet.

"Oh, Puppet. You said it! Jam! What a lovely word, and what a lovely thing! Jam it shall be!"

"Jam!"

Silvester laughed out loud. He carried Puppet to the steep stairs. He said goodbye to the spiders and woodlice and pigeons and mouse.

"Hold on tight," he said, and down they went.

In the living room, he held Puppet up before the photograph of Belinda.

"This is Belinda," he told him. "Belinda, this is Puppet.

I made him. He can walk and talk! Isn't he wonderful?"

He held Puppet so close that his nose touched the glass.

"Oh, how she would have loved you!" he exclaimed.

He showed Puppet the living room.

"That's a sofa and that's a chair, and that's a door and that's a wall. And… Gosh, you have so much to learn!"

He carried Puppet into the kitchen and sat him on the table. He heard the voices of children playing. Puppet turned his head towards the sound.

"It's just some children," said Silvester. "They must be in Holly Hill Park. It's not too far away. Perhaps you can meet them soon. Now then, where's that jam?"

"Jam!" said Puppet.

Silvester searched a cupboard.

"Ah, yes," he said. He took out a pot of jam and a loaf of bread. "This is bread; this is raspberry jam."

"Jam!"

Silvester cut a slice of bread and spread some jam on it.

"Look," he said. "This is what you do."

He lifted the bread and jam to his mouth and bit into it and chewed.

Puppet seemed to watch very, very carefully.

"It's delicious," said Silvester. "Mmm."

He held out the bread and jam to Puppet. Puppet stared at it.

"Your turn," said Silvester. "Go on."

He lifted Puppet's hand and pressed the bread and jam into it.

Puppet seemed to get the idea. He grabbed the bread and pushed it and squashed it against his mouth and rubbed it back and forward.

"Mmm!" he went. "Mmm. Mmm! Jam!"

Silvester laughed. "That's nearly right," he said. Then he pondered. "Maybe puppets don't eat anything at all."

"Mmm," went Puppet. "Jam!"

Silvester got a cloth and wiped away the red mess from Puppet's mouth. Then he took the corners of Puppet's mouth and lifted them.

"That's called smiling," he said. "You do it when you're happy."

Puppet smiled and smiled.

"Jam!" he said. "Mmm."

And Silvester smiled and smiled as well.

9

That Puppet! He was only made of wood and wire and paint, but he was so quick, so strong, so keen to be alive.

He walked in the kitchen. He walked in the living room. He got the idea of swinging his arms and legs in rhythm. He limped, he tottered in his lopsided way, but on he went, walking and smiling, smiling and walking.

"Such a wonderful lad!" said Silvester. He sat on a kitchen chair and drank some tea. "How can I keep up with you?" he wondered. "You'll wear me out!"

Puppet stopped and stood as if he was listening to the distant children again.

Silvester took him to the window.

Puppet spread his arms wide across the glass and gazed out. There was the narrow lane with the patch of sky above. At the end of the lane was the town square with its fountain and its benches and its shops and its cafes, and with the rest of the town spreading all around it.

It was all just a very short walk away.

"That's our town," Silvester told him. "That's the world. It's very lovely, Puppet."

He saw a woman and a girl walking hand in hand past the end of the lane, not a care in the world.

He lifted Puppet down and sat him on the windowsill. Puppet gazed out as if he was waiting for something.

Silvester looked at Puppet. He looked at the world outside.

Did he dare?

"Try this, Puppet," he said.

He led Puppet back into the living room and stood at his side.

"Hold my hand," he ordered. "Like this, look."

He reached down and took Puppet's left hand in his right.

"This is called holding hands, Puppet. Now we walk together, side by side."

He tugged gently at Puppet's hand, and Puppet walked beside him across the room. They couldn't get the rhythm right. They both stumbled.

Silvester groaned. "Who'd have thought something so simple could be so hard?" he muttered. "Let's try the other side."

He took Puppet's right hand in his left.

A little better.

They walked together step by step through the living room, through the kitchen and back again.

"Excellent!" said Silvester.

Then he went to the mirror on the kitchen wall. He licked his finger and smoothed his hair down. He ran his fingers across his face.

"Am I crazy?" he said to himself. "Is it too soon? Am I crazy?" he said to Belinda on the wall. He frowned. He grinned. "Maybe I am! So what?"

He straightened Puppet's clothes. He tugged the brown cap down over Puppet's forehead.

"Now listen," he said.

Puppet looked up at him.

"You must hold my hand and stay by my side. Do you understand?"

Puppet kept looking at him.

"Say yes, Dad," ordered Silvester.

"Jam!"

"Good boy. We'll be OK. We'll only be a little while. We'll go to the park, where the other children are."

Then he took a deep breath and opened the front door.

10

Silvester and Puppet stepped into the shadowy lane and headed towards the square. Puppet walked his limping, jaggedy walk. Silvester held his hand tight. They came into the sunlight. A group of men sat at a table outside Dragone's cafe. They were drinking coffee and playing cards.

"*Silvester?*" called one of the men.

Silvester paused.

"It is, isn't it?" said the man. "Silvester. The puppet man, yes?"

Silvester nodded. "Yes."

"Not seen you about for *ages*! Still doing the puppets?"

Silvester licked his lips. His heart was beating fast. "No, not now."

"Retired, eh? That's the style. He was a *wizard*," the man said to his friends. He pointed to the middle of the square. "You used to put your shows on here, *right here*, didn't you?"

Yes, they had done one or two small shows here, in the very early days. He and Belinda had put up a little make-shift stage, created from old curtains and scraps of wood. They had blown a little trumpet to announce themselves, and families and children had gathered round. That had all been long ago.

"You remember *that*?" Silvester asked.

"How could I forget? They were brilliant. *You* were brilliant. My kids were in hysterics!"

He leaned forward in his chair, peered at Puppet.

"Got a visitor, I see. Grandson, is it?"

"Yes," Silvester said quickly. He tugged at Puppet's hand.

"Name's Louis," said the man. "Care to join us?"

"N-no, thank you," said Silvester. "We're heading for the park."

"Best place for the lad. Another time, eh?"

"Yes."

Silvester led Puppet away.

"A total *wizard*," he heard Louis say to his friends.

His heart was thumping; his head was spinning.

"I'm remembered, Puppet," he said with wonder. "Of *course* I am."

Other people nodded and smiled. He and Puppet passed the ancient fountain. Silvester remembered the early makeshift shows here. In his mind he heard the little squeaky trumpet blown by Belinda. He heard himself as he had been way back then, calling out: "Gather round, the show's about to start!"

He laughed at himself, at the lovely memory.

An old couple on a bench whispered to each other. He heard his name. He heard a sigh.

"Of course I am remembered," he said again.

He held Puppet's hand tight. "That's a man," he told him. "A woman. A boy. A flower. A girl."

He almost tripped. Puppet stumbled with him, his limbs clicking and clacking. Some passer-by giggled out loud.

Maybe this was all too hard, Silvester thought. Maybe it was all too soon. He could turn around and just go home, but what good was that to a brand-new puppet who had to learn about the world?

They passed a long-haired busker sitting on the

grass, playing a guitar, swaying to his own music. Silvester dropped a coin into his hat and the busker raised his head and smiled.

"Keep going," Silvester said to Puppet. "Don't worry. We're just like any other granddad and his grandson."

Puppet didn't seem to be worrying at all.

There was a narrow road at the far end of the square.

"That's a car," Silvester said. "Another car. A bike. Oh, a bus!"

They came to a pedestrian crossing.

"We stand here," Silvester whispered. He pressed the button. His finger was trembling. "We wait for the green man. We wait for the traffic to stop. Then it's safe to cross and it's not much further to the park."

A police car pulled up. The officer in the passenger seat stared out at Puppet and Silvester.

Silvester swallowed. He stood still and held Puppet's hand tight but he wanted to run. He tried to look straight back into the police officer's eyes.

"Why do I feel guilty?" he whispered to himself. "I've done nothing wrong."

The officer wound the window down. "Everything all right, sir?" he asked.

"Yes, thank you," said Silvester.

"And the lad's OK?"

"Yes," said Silvester. "We're just going to the park."

The green man lit up. Silvester led Puppet across the road. The police officers watched. Silvester tried to smile at them.

A couple of kids rushed by. A boy leaned down and peered at Puppet, then looked up at Silvester.

He nudged his friend. They both made faces and sniggered and ran on.

The police car drove away.

"Just keep going," muttered Silvester. "If it's too much, we'll just go home again."

On they walked, along the pavement, towards the park, through the park gate.

A couple of families were picnicking on the grass. A few children were kicking a ball about. There were tall trees with shadows beneath and birds circling above. The day was warm and bright.

Puppet seemed to watch the people. He seemed to watch the birds flitting in and out of the trees. He turned up his face to the sun.

"Didn't I tell you it's a lovely world?" Silvester said.

Most folk took no notice of them. One or two smiled to see the puppet master from the past, or perhaps just a nice silver-haired old man and a nice if rather strange-looking boy.

Nothing more.

A small brown dog sniffed at Puppet's feet.

"Dog," explained Silvester. "Don't worry – it's just being friendly."

Puppet reached out to the dog and it licked his fingers.

"Jasper!" called someone. "Come here. Leave the poor little boy alone."

The dog trotted away.

"Little boy," echoed Silvester. "Did you hear, Puppet? *Little boy.*" He was calming down now. "Just relax," he said. "Take it easy, take your time. We're just like any other grand-dad and his grandson."

Music started up. It came from an ice-cream van beside a fenced-off swings park. Puppet tilted his head. Silvester smiled.

"Come along. We'll get you one of the loveliest things in the whole wide world."

Silvester licked his lips. He hadn't had an ice cream for years. When he had the puppet theatre, there'd always been ice cream at the interval.

Dream Ice Cream was written on the van in multi-coloured letters.

What should they have? There was a price list and pictures of lollies and treats.

"What shall I get you, Puppet?" asked Silvester. "A Space Rocket? A Magic Swirl? A Neapolitan?"

"Puppet?" came a voice from behind.

Silvester turned and saw a girl standing there.

"Is he *really* called Puppet?" she asked.

Silvester caught his breath. "Of course he isn't," he said. "He's called Kenneth."

Where on earth did that name come from?

"Kenneth?" said the girl.

"Yes."

The lady in the van leaned out of the hatch towards

them. "What can I get you?" she asked.

Silvester wanted to tell the lady that Puppet had never tasted ice cream before, but he knew how strange that would sound.

"Two vanilla cones, please," he said. "One for me, and one for Kenneth."

He smiled. It had to be vanilla, the best of all ice creams, the one he'd always loved when he was a little boy.

The lady smiled. She said, "Yes, of course."

"Hello, Kenneth," said the girl behind them.

Puppet said nothing.

She looked at him closely. "Is Kenneth all right?" she asked Silvester.

Silvester didn't answer. The lady handed him the vanilla cones.

"Was he in an accident?" asked the girl.

"Now then, madam," said the lady in the van. "That's not very nice, is it? Say you're sorry."

"I'm so sorry, Kenneth," said the girl.

She bought two vanilla cones too.

"My name's Fleur," she said. "I really am sorry."

Puppet stared back at her.

"He doesn't say much, does he?" she said to Silvester.

"No, he doesn't," admitted Silvester. "He's a quiet boy."

"Perhaps he's shy," she said. "That's all right, though, isn't it? My mum's a bit shy too." She waved at a woman sitting on a bench under a nearby tree. "Coming!" she called.

"I could draw a picture of him," she said to Silvester. "I've always got my sketchbook in my backpack. I like to find interesting subjects."

She peered at Puppet. He stared straight back at her.

"I don't think so," said Silvester. "But thank you. Goodbye, Fleur."

He led Puppet away, still holding both vanilla cones. Puppet stumbled and tottered and got up again. Silvester felt like he might totter over too.

"It's all right," he said. "She's gone. Let's sit here on the grass."

They sat down. The grass was warm.

Silvester gave Puppet his ice cream.

"You eat it," he said. "Like with the bread and jam."

"Jam!" said Puppet.

Puppet held the ice cream with both hands, stared at it, then tried to shove the whole thing into his mouth all at once.

"Slow down," warned Silvester. "You'll make yourself sick."

He tried to pull Puppet's hands away from his mouth but Puppet took no notice. He managed to smile even though his mouth was so full.

"Mmm!" he mumbled. "Mmm! Mmmmm!"

Then the ice cream spurted out of his mouth.

Silvester sighed. Ah, well. He licked his own ice cream.

Suddenly Puppet grabbed it and started trying to eat it too.

"No, Puppet, no!" cried Silvester.

Too late. The ice cream was all over Puppet's face. He smiled again and ice cream ran out of his mouth across his chin.

Silvester took out a tissue and started to wipe Puppet's face.

"Oh dear," he said. "I've got to teach you manners as well. And everything else a puppet has to know so that he can get on in the world."

He sighed. It was all such a responsibility. Would he be able to manage?

Fleur was sitting on the bench with her mum. She had an open sketchbook on her lap and a pencil in her hand. She waved. Silvester gave a little wave back.

A bunch of children walked past. They slowed right

down. They pretended not to look at Puppet, but they did, and they laughed.

Silvester glared at them and off they ran.

"Take no notice, Puppet," he said.

Puppet took no notice anyway. He looked through the fence towards the swings park. It was pretty quiet in there. Just a few young children and their parents. They swung back and forward on the squeaky swings and spun on the squeaky roundabout.

"That's called playing on the swings," Silvester told him.

He wiped the last of the ice cream from Puppet's face, and some of the green paint on Puppet's eyes flaked away with it.

"Oh dear," said Silvester. "I didn't make you properly, did I?" He sighed again. "Maybe we should get back now and smarten you up and come again another day."

But Puppet was looking at the swings park.

"A turn on the swings," Silvester said. "That's what children like to do. Is that a good idea?"

Puppet seemed to think it was. He was already setting off.

11

So into the swings park they went. Silvester lifted Puppet onto a swing and showed him how to hold the chains, then pushed him back and forward, back and forward. The chains squeaked beautifully, in rhythm with the swing.

Puppet soon got the hang of leaning forward and back to keep the movement going. Swinging there, he looked just like any young boy.

"Look at you!" said Silvester. "How quick and clever you are!"

Silvester pushed and Puppet swung, back and forward, up and down, back and forward, up and down. He pushed again and pushed again, and he loved the rhythm and ease of it.

A little boy climbed on the swing next to Puppet's. The boy's mum started pushing him.

"Hello," she said to Silvester.

"Hello," said Silvester back.

"It's a nice day, isn't it?" she added.

"It certainly is," Silvester agreed.

"He's your grandson?"

Silvester blinked. "Who is?"

"Him."

"Oh, yes. Sorry. His name is Kenneth."

"This is Tom. Say hello to Kenneth, Tom."

Tom just scowled. Perhaps he didn't want to say hello to anybody today.

"Higher!" he said.

"Children, eh?" said his mum. "He's in one of his moods today," she whispered to Silvester.

She pushed Tom higher. Silvester pushed Puppet higher.

"And how old is Kenneth?" asked the woman.

"Seven," said Silvester very quickly. He caught his breath. Time to leave, he thought.

"Tom is four," she said. "Which school is Kenneth at?"

School? Did Puppet go to school? Silvester's heart started thumping. He shoved harder. Puppet held on tight.

"He hasn't been there much recently," he said after a pause. "He's been rather poorly."

"Poor lad. I thought he looked a bit…"

"Yes. He's getting over it now, thank goodness."

"And which school?"

"Which school?"

"Yes. Which school does Kenneth go to?"

"Oh. That nice one. St Giles."

"Oh. I don't know that one."

"Neither do I," muttered Silvester.

He pushed harder. Puppet kicked his feet and held on tighter.

"Higher!" demanded Tom.

"Jam!" shouted Puppet.

"Hold on tight!" said Tom's mother.

Silvester pushed harder.

"Does he like it?" asked Tom's mother.

"Like what?"

"Like St Giles?"

"Oh yes. Very much."

Silvester pushed even harder. Far too hard. Puppet wasn't holding on tight enough and he flew off the swing and into the air and landed with a clatter on the ground.

"Oh no!" screamed Tom's mother. She was quicker than Silvester and she reached Puppet first. "Oh, Kenneth!" she gasped. "Oh, just look at you!"

His limbs were splayed in the weirdest way.

"We need to call an ambulance!" she exclaimed.

"No!" said Silvester.

"What?"

"He'll be all right. He's very flexible."

Silvester crouched beside Puppet. He started to rear-range his limbs.

"See?" he said. "He'll be fine now."

Tom's mum touched Puppet's cheek. She touched his wrist. She clapped her hand to her mouth.

"He's cold!" she cried. "He must be—"

"That's how he always is," said Silvester. He's very cold-blooded."

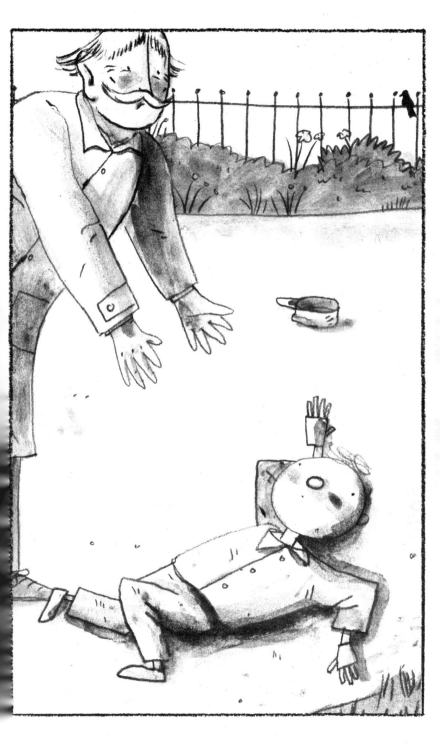

"Speak to us, Kenneth," urged the woman. "Say something."

"Jam!" mumbled Puppet.

The woman looked at Silvester. "Jam?"

"Raspberry. He's very fond of it."

Silvester took Puppet's hands and helped him to his feet. He picked his cap up from where it had fallen and put it back on Puppet's head. "No harm done," he said. "Fit as a fiddle."

"Are you certain?" said Tom's mum. "He still looks a little… In fact, he looks *very*…"

"He often looks like that. Come along, Puppet. Kenneth! We'll get going." He held Puppet's hand.

Tom stood in the way. Puppet kicked him in the shin.

"Kenneth!" cried Silvester.

Tom's mum pulled her son away. "What's he *doing*?"

"He's confused," said Silvester. "He's in one of his moods."

She glared. "One of his *moods*?"

"Yes. Just like your Tom."

Puppet swung his foot again, like he was getting ready to kick Tom a second time. Silvester held him back.

"What a little monster!" exclaimed Tom's mum.

Puppet swung his foot at her.

Silvester drew him gently away. "Children, eh?" he said. "Come along, Pupp— Kenneth! Let's leave these people alone."

They tottered together out of the swings park.

"I hope we never see you here again!" yelled Tom's mum.

"Little monsta!" shouted Tom in a high-pitched voice.

"Oh dear," sighed Silvester. "Maybe you aren't made for this cruel world, my little Puppet. Home. Let's go home."

And so they left, hand in hand, tottering homewards.

"Monsta!" shouted Tom again. "Little monsta!"

12

"Is Kenneth all right?"

Fleur appeared at Silvester's side as they left the swings park.

"Yes, thank you," said Silvester. He and Puppet kept on walking.

"We saw him flying off the swing," she said, walking alongside them.

"He's fine now," said Silvester. "Don't worry about him."

"Would you like to come and sit with us? My mum would love to meet you again."

"Again?" said Silvester.

He looked towards Fleur's mum. There she was, sitting in the shade under the tree.

"She saw you long ago," Fleur explained. "She says you used to have a puppet theatre."

Silvester smiled. "Another time, perhaps," he said. He felt so tired. It had all been a bit much. "I need to get Kenneth home."

"She says it was wonderful," added Fleur.

Silvester looked at Fleur's mum again. She waved. He gave a little wave back.

"Did Kenneth use to help with the theatre?" asked Fleur.

Silvester shook his head. "How could he? He's far too young."

"How old *is* he?" said Fleur. She carried on walking at their side. "He looks…"

"Looks *what*?" said Silvester. He wanted to tell her to go away, to leave them alone, but he knew she was just interested.

"Looks like he could be very old."

Silvester paused.

"And like he could be very young as well," Fleur added.

Silvester looked at her. Puppet stood dead still and looked at her too.

"How could that be?" Silvester asked her.

"I don't know."

Silvester smiled again.

"To tell the truth," said Fleur, "sometimes *I* feel like that."

"Like what?"

"Like I'm very young and very old, all at the same time. But I'm actually ten."

Silvester blinked and laughed. "To tell the truth," he said, "so do I!"

And they stood together in the park for a few silent moments and looked at one another: the puppet master, the puppet and the girl.

Fleur crouched down beside Puppet. She tenderly touched his head.

"It must have been so frightening for you," she said, "flying off the swing like that."

"Jam."

"Yes. Jam. Frightening things happen to us all, but we get over them."

"Jam."

Silvester watched and listened. He didn't try to draw Puppet away. He didn't mind that this girl was touching his wooden head, his wooden feet. He had the strangest feeling that Fleur was meant to be in the park today. Perhaps she and Silvester and Puppet were destined to meet.

"Thank you for your kindness, Fleur," he said.

"I'm only being friendly. The world is difficult for Kenneth, isn't it?"

"Difficult?"

She gently touched Puppet's three-fingered hand. "It is for all of us sometimes, I think."

"Yes," agreed Silvester. "It is."

He gazed at her. She was like so many children that he'd known, so many children whose understanding surpasses that of many adults.

"How do you do it?" she asked him.

Silvester frowned. "Do what?"

"My mum says you were like a magician. You could do anything."

Silvester smiled. "Does she?"

"Yes. She says she's never forgotten." She touched Puppet's black-booted foot. "Would you show me how to do it?"

"How to do what?"

"How to make puppets."

Silvester laughed. "It's easy," he said. "Anything at all can become a puppet."

"Anything?"

"Yes."

He looked down at the ground. There were twigs and pebbles, leaves and grass. He picked up a small Y-shaped twig and held it between his fingers. He moved it across the grass as if it had two legs.

"Left, right, left, right," he said. "Look. It's walking. It's alive."

They looked together at this thing that suddenly did almost seem to have a life of its own. Silvester lifted it and turned it towards Fleur.

"My name is Twiglet," he made it say in a twiggish voice. *"Hello, Fleur."*

"Hello, Twiglet," she replied.

She widened her eyes. She picked up an oval-shaped stone and held it between her fingers. She made it speak.

"My name is Stone. Hello, Twiglet."

"Hello, Stone," the twig replied.

"See?" said Silvester. "The world is filled with puppets."

He let the twig fall back onto the grass.

"It's magic!" said Fleur.

"Yes," agreed Silvester. "Yet it's just twigs and stones and voices and not difficult at all."

They laughed together at the strangeness of it.

Then Silvester felt tired again. He said they really had to go.

"Will I see you again?" asked Fleur. "Will I see Kenneth again?"

Silvester didn't know.

"You could come and visit us," said Fleur. "We could have tea and make puppets in the garden."

Silvester nodded. "Perhaps we could." He realized he would like that.

"Would you like that, Kenneth?" asked Fleur.

"Jam!"

"That means yes, doesn't it?" she said.

"It does," agreed Silvester.

"We live in a place called Crow Hall."

"Crow Hall?"

Fleur laughed. "Well, it's not much of a hall. It's more like a battered old cottage."

"It sounds lovely."

"It is! And the garden's more like a wilderness than a garden. But it's very peaceful and lovely in its own way."

Silvester smiled. "I'm sure it is," he said.

"We're trying to bring it all back to life again."

"And are you managing to do that?"

"Yes. We're starting to."

"That's good."

Silvester looked down at Puppet. "Would you like to see Fleur again?" he asked.

"Jam!" said Puppet.

Fleur quickly ran to her mum and just as quickly ran back again.

"Mum says come any time. How about tomorrow?"

"Tomorrow? OK, tomorrow."

She wrote the address and drew a little map on a sheet of paper and gave it to him.

Silvester led Puppet away.

"Bye-bye, Kenneth!" Fleur called.

Puppet turned to look back at her.

He waved.

13

Silvester and Puppet left the park, crossed the road and headed back across the square.

Outside Dragone's cafe, the men were still sitting at the table with their coffee and their cards.

"Hello again," called Louis.

Silvester nodded.

"Had a good time?"

"Yes, thank you."

"The young 'un looks a bit worse for wear."

The men at the table all leaned over to look at Puppet.

Silvester looked at him too. Face all scratched and scraped. Clothes torn where he had fallen off the swing. One of his legs was even more wonky.

"Yes," he said. "He has been in the wars today."

"It can be tough sometimes, being young," said Louis. "Would he like a biscuit? There's a couple left over here."

Silvester shook his head. "No, thank you. Best get him home, I think."

"Bath and a mug of hot chocolate, maybe."

"Something like that," agreed Silvester. "He's called Kenneth, by the way."

"Nice to meet you, Kenneth. I'm Louis."

He put out his hand. Puppet just looked at it.

"Nice to meet you," Louis said again.

"Jam!" said Puppet.

Louis smiled kindly. "Enjoy your bath, son. And your hot chocolate."

"Come along, Kenneth," said Silvester. "Let's get you home."

And homewards they walked.

14

Poor Puppet. Poor Silvester.

Both worn out.

Silvester sprawled on the sofa with Puppet tucked in at his side.

"Poor you," Silvester said. "You really *have* been in the wars."

Puppet didn't move.

"But we made a friend. Fleur. Remember?"

Puppet didn't move, didn't speak. Silvester gently tapped his head.

"Puppet?"

No answer.

"Puppet. Is it over already, Puppet?"

Silvester tapped himself on the head. Maybe he'd been asleep all this time.

Maybe all of this had been just a dream.

He looked at the picture of Belinda on the wall.

"He's just wood and wire and wax and paint," he said to her. "How on earth can he be alive?"

She gazed back at him with gentle brown eyes.

"Or maybe life just comes and goes," he said. "Ah, well."

He took a scrapbook from a shelf. He sat on the sofa and turned its pages. So many photographs: dozens of old puppet shows, hundreds of old puppets. Newspaper cuttings and reviews. Letters from people around the world. The best of them were from children, saying how much they'd laughed, how they'd been terrified, how they'd felt sad, and how they'd laughed and laughed and laughed again.

Sometimes the children had sent little puppets that they had made themselves.

"We were a force for good in the world," he said to Belinda in the photograph. "Weren't we, my love?"

Yes, she whispered, from long ago. *Yes, my love, we were.*

And Puppet stirred.

"Puppet?" said Silvester.

Puppet looked up at him.

"Hello again," Silvester softly said. "I thought you might

have gone away." He turned the pages of the book. "Have a look at this! This was our van."

There it was, the old van, in an ancient photograph.

The name was written in bright multicoloured letters across its side:

SILVESTER'S MAGICAL PUPPET THEATRE

Around the words were pictures of puppets, all bright and alive, dancing and dangling, grinning and snarling.

"And look, Puppet. This is me, with my beautiful Belinda at my side."

There they were together, in front of the van, with sunlight pouring down on them. Silvester had long dark hair. He wore a top hat, and a bright satin waistcoat decorated with stars and comets and moons. A puppet dangled from strings in his hand. Belinda wore a long tight sky-blue dress. She had on a yellow necklace and bright red earrings, and she held a dancing puppet too.

Both of them so young and free, so full of life.

Puppet watched as the pages turned.

"You'd have loved it. And we'd have loved to have you with us, there in the van! We went everywhere. Cities and villages and theatres and country fairs. We did the shows on riverbanks and beaches and in marketplaces and schools and children's homes. Everywhere we went, they cheered and clapped. Everywhere, they laughed and screamed and gasped and cried."

Silvester closed his eyes, drifted through time, present to past and back again.

He smiled at himself. "Sorry, Puppet. Keep going off to dreamland."

He turned more pages.

"The children fell in love with the show. They'd move like puppets, dance like puppets, talk as if they were puppets themselves. And the adults? They turned into children again for an hour or so in their busy and troubled lives."

Another page.

There was the van in front of a dark stone building with great steel heavy gates.

"That's a prison, Puppet. Once or twice we performed in there, in that dark and dour and desolate place. We performed for men who had done the wickedest deeds. And they laughed and cried like they were little boys again."

Silvester pointed to a picture of a great muscular man with tattoos of snakes on his cheeks.

"Ah yes. Frederick. As the warders led him back to his cell, he leaned over to me and whispered, 'You released me, Silvester. Thank you. My name is Frederick. You made me free.'"

Silvester turned the pages and turned the pages.

"How strange," he said. "These things happened long before you came to life, when you were just bits and pieces on a bench upstairs. And now Belinda's at rest, the van conked out and was turned to scrap, and all the puppets have gone to the museum."

He shrugged and smiled. "Now it's just me and you."

A little paper puppet slid out from between the pages into Puppet's lap.

Silvester picked it up. There was a label tied to it.

Thank you for the show. His name is Claude. With love from Antonia.

Two lengths of thread were attached to Claude's hands.

"Hello, Claude!" said Silvester. "What a nice surprise."

He showed Puppet how to use the threads to move Claude's hands. Puppet tried to copy him, and Silvester helped. Puppet moved Claude's legs, held Claude up to his face, looked into Claude's little pencilled eyes, touched Claude's crayoned cheeks. On his pocket was written a faded letter C.

"Say hello, Claude," said Silvester.

"Hello."

Puppet played. He moved Claude from side to side through the empty air. He made him fly. He made him dance.

"Ha ha, Puppet," laughed Silvester. "You're a puppeteer too!"

And they played like that as the sky darkened and evening approached.

And they came to rest.

✦ ✦ ✦

Later, Silvester inspected Puppet's scratched cheek. He looked at his torn clothes, his scrawny hair.

"We need to fix you up," he decided. "We're seeing Fleur again tomorrow, and we need her and the world to see how beautiful and strong you really are. Don't we?"

"Jam!"

An owl hooted somewhere.

"That's an owl," Silvester said. "It comes at night. Say 'hello, owl'."

"E-O," said Puppet.

They sat quietly as the silvery light shone in on them. A baby cried somewhere and then quietened.

"And sleep," Silvester said softly. "Sleep comes at night as well. It's when we close our eyes and disappear from the world. Sleep, Puppet. Sleep. Close your eyes, my little one. Night-night."

And Silvester closed his eyes and slept, there on the sofa with Puppet at his side.

And Puppet became still as timber, still as stone, with little Claude lying against his chest.

15

Deep into the night, Silvester woke and carried Puppet up the steep stairs.

The moon shone in through the window to the sky.

He laid Puppet on the workbench.

He switched on the desk light.

He took Claude from Puppet's arms and carefully laid him beside him on the bench.

An owl hooted. A cat yowled. A moth came, fluttering in the lamplight. And another. A mouse scuttled on the floor. And here came the dangling spiders, and the dark woodlice at the edges of the bench.

"Hello, everyone!" Silvester whispered. He laughed. "You'll never guess what happened to this little lad today!"

He told them everything. The mouse squeaked. The moth fluttered.

"And look at the mess of him now," he said sadly. He stroked Puppet's cheek. "I'm sorry, Puppet," he whispered. "I haven't taken enough care with you."

He shook his head. "I didn't realize what I was really

doing, Puppet. I didn't realize that you would come to *life*!"

He talked to the spiders and he laughed out loud.

"I didn't realize he would come to *life*!"

He lifted a piece of sandpaper and, very gently, he sanded the scratches on Puppet's face. He smoothed Puppet's body, arms and legs.

And all through the rest of that night, beneath the lamp and the moon, Silvester worked to make Puppet the best puppet it was possible for him to be. He tightened Puppet's joints. He reshaped Puppet's face. He smoothed and waxed his skin. He thickened Puppet's hair. He brightened his green eyes.

As he worked, his body relaxed; his mind relaxed. He was like the old Silvester, the bold magician of the puppet theatre. He was like the little boy making his first puppets to show to his mam.

He remembered how nothing ever seemed quite fixed. He might start off making a boy but find himself making a girl. Making a queen that became a king. Making a cat that became a dog. He loved the way the puppets would move and shift between his hands, the way all puppets would seem to seek their own true shape, the way they really did seem to seek true life.

This would be Silvester's final puppet; he knew that. Puppet was brand new, but he was made from bits of ancient puppets, scraps and fragments, stuff that seemed nearly useless. He was, as Fleur had said, both young and old. He had bits of Silvester in him, bits of Belinda, bits of memories, bits of dream. He had grown from all the puppets that had gone before, and he would lead to all the puppets that were still to come.

When Silvester was done, he smiled.

Yes, Puppet was still odd and twisted, a funny-looking thing.

No, he would never be perfect, but he was beautiful.

He was beautiful and imperfect, as all the most beautiful things are.

Silvester dressed him anew: black cotton trousers, a black cotton top with pockets, the kind of simple clothes he'd given to so many of his puppets in the past. He put a blue cap on Puppet's head. He tucked Claude into Puppet's breast pocket.

"You look wonderful, my little Puppet," said Silvester. "You truly are the puppet that you were meant to be."

He laid him carefully back on the bench.

Then the spiders dangled closer and all the little creatures watched as Silvester lowered his head and slept again.

16

Silvester stirred. He rubbed his eyes and yawned.

Puppet lay beside him, bathed in daylight. Claude lay in Puppet's pocket.

"Puppet?" Silvester whispered.

Puppet didn't move.

He tried again. "Puppet?"

Nothing.

He held Puppet by the shoulders and stood him on the bench.

"You look so splendid," he said.

He let go and Puppet clattered to the bench. He tried again and Puppet fell a second time.

"Is it time to put strings on you?"

Nothing.

Silvester sighed. "Perhaps it is," he said. "Perhaps it's all been just an illusion."

He searched for a box and found it. Inside were many tiny sharp hooks. He took out five of them and wiped them clean. One for each hand, one for each knee, one for the top of Puppet's head.

He searched again and found an ancient cross-shaped piece of wood that the strings would dangle from.

He picked up one of the hooks and tested it against his own skin. Yes, sharp enough.

He took a deep breath. He paused, then pressed its point against the back of Puppet's left hand and began to turn.

Puppet flinched. He opened his eyes.

Silvester gave a sigh of relief. He took the hook away.

"Hello," he said.

"E-O," said Puppet.

"I stopped believing in you for a moment," admitted Silvester. "Please forgive me."

"Jam."

Silvester stared into Puppet's bright green eyes. "Did I hurt you?"

"Jam."

"And am I cruel, to bring you back again?"

"Jam."

"This is the world. Do you remember? I am Silvester. We're off to see our friends today. We're going to visit their garden. Do you remember?"

No answer.

Silvester frowned. Was it cruel to bring these sticks to life again? Should he have left Puppet as he was, just scattered fragments lying in the dust?

But Puppet struggled to his feet. He took Claude from his pocket and held him in both hands and gazed at him.

"E-O," he said.

Claude said nothing, of course. He didn't stir.

Silvester carried them both down the steep stairs to the kitchen. He made tea and bread and jam and they breakfasted together. Puppet swiped the jam across his mouth and went "Mmm, mmm." He touched some jam to Claude's mouth too and went *"Mmm, mmm"* as if Claude were speaking.

Silvester laughed. "Puppet the puppeteer!" he exclaimed.

After breakfast he had a bath and shaved his stubble. He trimmed his hair. He got out some clothes he hadn't worn for years: a pair of blue jeans, a blue shirt with white birds on it.

He looked at himself in the mirror.

"Not quite as you used to be," he said. "But better than you were just yesterday."

He lifted Puppet and held him up to the mirror too.

"That is me and that is you," he said. "Look how smart we are!"

He waved, and Silvester in the mirror waved too.

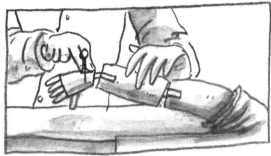

He lifted Puppet's hand and made it wave, and the puppet in the mirror waved too.

Puppet craned forward in Silvester's arms until his nose almost touched the mirror.

"Do you understand?" asked Silvester. "That is both of us, reflected back."

Puppet swung his right leg and kicked, and his hard little foot struck the wall.

Silvester laughed. "No," he said. "It's you, Puppet. It's you with me. There's no need to be scared. They're called reflections."

Puppet leaned again, closer, closer. Then he held up Claude, and there was Claude in the mirror too.

He moved Claude as if he were flying, and Claude in the mirror flew too.

They all gazed into and out from the mirror, the three faces.

"Don't we look wonderful?" Silvester said.

Then he turned them all away.

"Right, we have a garden to get to, my lovely friends," he said. "Are you prepared?"

"Jam," said Puppet. "Jam."

17

The men were sitting in the square again, outside Dragone's, bathed in morning light.

"You're in much better fettle today," said Louis. "What a dapper pair you are!"

"Indeed we are!" Silvester agreed.

"One could almost think you're off to set up a puppet show."

"Oh no, those days are long, long gone. We're off to see some friends today."

"Lucky you, and lucky friends."

Louis swigged his coffee and leaned towards Puppet.

"On a day such as this," he said, "the whole world is a splendid thing! Don't you agree, Kenneth?"

"Jam!"

"Precisely. Jam! There couldn't be a truer word! What a brilliant mind you have!"

On they walked. Puppet limped; he swayed; he skipped along.

Like any grandfather, any grandson, thought Silvester.

At the far side of the square, there was a butcher's shop named simply Meat.

Puppet clattered to a halt outside it and turned his face towards the mounds of sausages, the slices of steak, the trays of chops. The butcher himself stood just inside, in a red and white apron and a bright red hap, his arms folded across his belly.

"That," Silvester said, "is meat." He poked his own belly. "It's what I'm made from, I suppose."

He felt he should tell Puppet about bones and skin and flesh and blood and how they come together to make bodies, and talk about the bodies of humans and the bodies of other beasts, but the butcher was watching them. He leaned across the sausages and chops. His huge face came closer to the window. He stared at the old man out there, and at the young boy by his side. His jaw dropped, as if he'd never seen anything like this before. He stood up tall and gritted his teeth and glared.

"Get lost!" he yelled.

Silvester backed away. He held Puppet's hard little wooden hand tight and they moved on.

Outside Lisette's Barbershop, they paused again. Inside, a young woman – it must be Lisette herself, thought Silvester – gracefully moved around a boy in a chair. She happily snip-snipped with scissors while pop music played, and the boy's dad waited in an armchair by the wall.

"That's called having a haircut," explained Silvester. "It's hairdressing."

Lisette was dark-haired with bright flashing eyes. She turned and waved and beckoned them in.

Silvester smiled. "Not today, thank you!" he called.

"Perhaps another time!" she called back.

"Perhaps." He sighed and led Puppet away.

Oh, wouldn't it be so nice – to take Puppet into such a place, to sit by the wall and to flick through a newspaper while Puppet had his hair cut?

"Never to be," he murmured to himself. "Ah, well."

On they went.

Silvester named objects and places, and Puppet seemed to listen and look.

What did Puppet hear? What did Puppet see? His hard little feet tap-tapped on the earth as he moved along. Limbs softly clicked and softly clacked.

A cat appeared, a little black cat with shining eyes and a curving tail and lovely white paws.

"Cat," said Silvester.

He crouched right down and stroked the creature, and its fur was so beautiful, so warm, so soft.

"This is a cat, Puppet," he said. "It is a lovely thing." He rested his whole hand on the cat, and felt its breath, its beating heart. "You see the beauty of it?"

He took Puppet's hand and rested it beside his.

"You feel the life in it?"

The cat purred and they felt the vibration of the purr.

"Such a miracle," Silvester said.

The cat stretched its legs and arched its back. Silvester felt as if he'd never seen a cat before.

"Felix!" came a child's voice. "Felix! Felix!"

And the cat left them, leaping across the square towards a little girl.

"His name is Felix, Puppet," said Silvester. "Just look how he runs!"

And now another voice called out, "Would you care for a taste, sir?"

They were outside a cake shop. Its name was written across its window in gold: Cakes of Heaven.

Behind the window were trays of cupcakes. A multi-tiered wedding cake. A cake in the shape of a ship and one in the shape of an elephant. There were muffins, meringues and macaroons. Above the cakes were sugar-icing angels, dangling from strings.

A man stood at the door with a tray in his hand. He had red hair and wore a green apron with a picture of a yellow mixing bowl upon it.

"Would you like one, sir?" he asked, holding out a tray with little cubes of cake on it. "Orange cake today. Very tasty if I may say so myself. Take a piece, and you too, my bonny lad."

Silvester took a piece.

"Nice?" asked the man.

"Delicious," said Silvester.

"Excellent. And you, young man?"

"Jam!" said Puppet.

The man smiled. "Aha! I should have known!" And in he went, and out he came with a jam tart in his hand.

Puppet looked, and he took the tart and smeared it across his mouth and sighed, "Mmm! Mmm! Mmm!"

Silvester tried to apologize but the man just laughed.

"We each love cakes in our different ways!" he said. "The name's Laurence, by the way."

"I'm Silvester and this is Kenneth."

"And how are you spending this lovely day?"

"We're off to see some friends."

"You should take a box of cakes with you!"

Silvester nodded. "Of course we should!"

In Laurence went again, and out he came with a blue box tied with a golden ribbon. *Cakes of Heaven* was written in gold on the box.

"A selection of our best," he said.

Silvester held out a banknote. Laurence bowed and took it from him.

"I have discovered," he said, "that those with a fondness for cakes are often those with the strongest imaginations."

"Are they really?" said Silvester.

"Yes. And you look like a man of imagination. As does

young Kenneth. So let me ask you a question."

"Is it a hard one?" wondered Silvester.

"Not for one with a mind like yours. Here it is. Have you thought that the world itself is like cake?"

Silvester nibbled at the remnants of the orange cake.

"I must admit that I have not," he said.

Silvester pondered. He tapped his cheek. Puppet gazed at a crow that swooped overhead.

"Those houses there with their risen roofs," said Laurence, "are they not like fruit cakes just out of the oven?"

Silvester looked towards the houses at the far side of the square.

"And those distant hills beyond the roofs," continued Laurence. "They're like muffins and teacakes. And little rock cakes are scattered everywhere. And the sky above is like blue icing and the clouds are like cream…"

Silvester laughed. He opened his eyes and his imagination wide.

"It's like I've never seen the world before!" he said.

Puppet skipped.

"And look," said Laurence. "The sun above is just a custard tart!"

"It is!" exclaimed Silvester. "Of course it is! I've never seen the sun before!"

"But for you, young Kenneth, it must be a jam tart, and its jam is apricot."

Puppet skipped again.

"Jam, jam!" he said.

Silvester laughed again. "Thank you so much, Laurence."

"You're most welcome. Enjoy your picnic. Give my blessings – and my cakes – to your dear friends."

"We will!"

And on they went, under the custard sun and the icing sky.

18

The pair soon came to a little housing estate. Somebody was playing a guitar somewhere. Puppet moved his feet and swung his body in time with it.

"Clever Puppet," Silvester said. "This is called music. It pours from the air into your mind and moves your bones."

Two boys lay on a patch of green, heads resting on their hands as they stared into the sky.

"Do you believe in them, mister?" said one to Silvester as he passed by.

"Believe in what?" he replied.

The boy sat up. "In ghosts."

"I'm not sure," said Silvester. "Do you?"

"There was one in my bedroom just last night."

"No, there wasn't," said his friend.

"Yes, there was. It spoke to me and said in a spooky voice, 'I have come to get you, Malcolm Molloy.'"

"He's making it up," said the other boy.

Malcolm laughed. "No, I'm not. I was petrified."

He jumped up and clenched his fists and punched the air.

"And it was just about to get me, and then I said, 'Get lost, ghost!' And off it went."

"What a load of rubbish," said his friend.

"No, it's not. The world's a lot weirder than you think it is, mate!" Malcolm glanced at Puppet. "Do *you* believe in ghosts?"

Puppet said nothing, of course, but he tilted his head as if he was listening.

"They're spirits," Malcolm said. "They look like they're alive but they're dead. They look like they've got bodies but you can see through them and they can walk through walls and—"

He clapped his hand across his mouth.

"I'm sorry," he said to Silvester. "He's just a kid. I'm scaring him."

His friend sighed. "He makes stuff up, mister, all the time."

Malcolm gasped in horror and pointed across the street.

"There it is again! And it's coming to get you, Billy! Aargh!"

Billy couldn't help looking. His eyes were wide with fright, then he jumped on Malcolm and they started to roar with laughter and wrestle on the grass.

"It always ends like this," said Billy, wiping snot from his face. "Dunno why I put up with him."

"Because I'm your best mate," said Malcolm. "Aargh, no, it's coming again!"

They fought again.

Silvester and Puppet walked on.

"Those were boys, Puppet," said Silvester. "And that was a story that might be true or might be false, and it doesn't matter either way."

An older girl and a boy leaned against a low garden wall, reading books.

"They're turning words into stories inside their heads," Silvester said. "It's like magic!" he added.

A teenage boy and a teenage girl sat arm in arm beneath a tree, smiling and whispering to each other.

"That's love," Silvester said. "That's a kind of magic too."

A laughing woman called from somewhere, "It happens every time! Get that daft dog out of here."

A baby in a pram outside an open front door waved its arms towards the sky.

"That's a baby," whispered Silvester. "It came from a mother and a father. It will grow into another child."

Puppet swayed.

"Then it will become a teenager," said Silvester. "Then an adult. And it might have children of its own. Then it will become an old person like me. And then…"

He shook his head. "So much magic, Puppet!" he cried. "So many stories! Such an astonishing world!"

He opened his eyes and his heart and his imagination wide.

"It's true! It's like I've never seen the world before!"

On they wandered, on and on, past the people, past the houses, through narrow streets, through voices, stories, music and songs.

Silvester kept on naming, naming.

"*House* and *wall* and *tree* and *road*. *Grass* and *sun* and *sky*."

He suddenly laughed.

"It's like scenery, Puppet!" he said. "The whole world is the scenery in the puppet theatre!"

He laughed and laughed.

"The whole world is a stage. And we walk on it and talk on it."

"Jam!" said Puppet.

"We're acting out a play, Puppet! And its name is…" He pondered. "Yes! *Puppet and Silvester in the Big Wide World*."

"Jam!" said Puppet again.

"Yes," said Silvester. "That's another title. A better title, Puppet! *Jam! Jam! Jam! The Tale of Jam!*"

They moved on.

Still the guitar player played.

Still the children read.

Still the woman laughed about the dog.

Still the teenagers whispered.

Still Malcolm and Billy wrestled and laughed.

And Puppet's feet tap-tapped on the earth. Limbs softly clicked and softly clacked.

On he walked, as if blood ran through his wooden limbs and breath flowed through his wooden lungs.

As if a little heart was beating hard inside his wooden chest.

"Oh, my Puppet," Silvester said. "You make me glad to be alive!"

19

Soon, here it was. *Crow Hall* was painted roughly on an old wooden gate set into a high stone wall. The gate had rusty steel hinges and a big black door knocker.

Silvester banged it hard.

No answer.

He banged again.

No answer.

"Maybe we'll come back another day," he said.

But then a voice called from inside. "Can I help you?" It was Fleur.

Silvester leaned close to the gate.

"It's Silvester and Kenneth," he said. "We met yesterday, if you remember," he added.

No answer.

"If it's too much bother, we'll just go away again."

The gate creaked open a few centimetres and there was Fleur, pulling hard from the other side.

"Hello!" she said. "You came! Push!"

Silvester pushed the gate hard with his shoulder. Puppet kicked hard with his little foot.

"Mum!" Fleur called. "They're here! Come and help!"

Puppet kicked, Silvester pushed, Fleur pulled. The hinges creaked and the gate scraped the earth.

"It hasn't been opened for years," explained Fleur.

Now Fleur's mum was there too, pulling along with Fleur. They all puffed and panted.

The gate opened just wide enough for Silvester and Puppet to squeeze through. Then they all leaned on the gate to shut it again.

"Sorry it was so stiff," said Fleur.

"We always come in the back way," added her mum.

Fleur laughed. "Oh, aren't you both so smart! Kenneth, you look wonderful."

"We thought we should look our best for you," Silvester said shyly.

"And you do!"

"Welcome to Crow Hall," said her mum.

Fleur laughed again. "It's not a hall at all, is it?" she said.

It was not. Just an old tumbledown cottage with a sagging roof and pink roses growing around the windows. The garden was a wilderness. Long grasses and wild flowers. There were trees with ancient pathways curving through them. A couple of great oak trees with branches twisting and spreading into the sky. One huge thick horizontal branch was almost as wide as the garden itself.

"Please, sit down," said Fleur's mum.

They all sat on chairs around a table on the grass beside the cottage.

"This is so exciting!" exclaimed Fleur. "Would you like some tea?"

"We would," said Silvester. "And we brought some cakes!"

Fleur hurried into the house.

It was warm behind the garden wall. It felt so separate from the world outside. Bees buzzed and butterflies danced. Birds flickered and sang in the trees. Not far from the table was a pond with the glint of golden fish in it.

"It's lovely here!" said Silvester.

"Yes," said Fleur's mum. "No one seemed to want it until we came along. Too much work, I suppose. My name is Antonia, by the way."

Fleur came out with a tray of tea, and Silvester opened the box of cakes.

"Cakes of Heaven," said Antonia. "They're the best."

"Jam!" cried Puppet. He grabbed a jam tart and smeared it across his mouth.

"He doesn't have very good manners, I'm afraid," Silvester said.

Fleur poured the tea. "We're bringing the garden to life again, aren't we, Mum?" she said.

"We've been trying to," agreed Antonia. "It's quite a task."

"*Jak!*" called a bird. It was a jackdaw, perching on the long horizontal oak tree branch.

"*Jak!*" it went again. "*Jak!*"

"Hello, Jack!" said Antonia. "He's very tame. And so intelligent."

"*Jak!*"

"This is Silvester," Fleur said to the bird. "And this is his grandson, Kenneth."

Puppet stood beneath the branch and looked up.

"*Jak!*" went the jackdaw.

"*Jak!*" went Puppet. "*Jak! Jak! Jak!*"

Antonia smiled. "You're making a friend!"

The jackdaw flew up into the air then fluttered back down onto the branch. It did it again. Puppet flapped his arms as if they were wings. He stood high and stretched upward, as if about to fly.

"Maybe I should have put wings on you, my Puppet,"

Silvester said. He caught his breath, surprised at his own words. "Kenneth, I mean."

Antonia laughed. "Wouldn't we all like to fly?" She spread her own arms and flapped them gently. "And maybe we will, one day."

Another jackdaw came and sat on the branch beside the first.

There were bigger birds, crows and ravens. And little finches dashing back and forth. The air was filled with their fluttering and with the roughness of their calls, the sweetness of their songs.

Silvester, Antonia and Fleur sat for a moment in the dappled light beneath the tree. Silvester breathed deeply. He hadn't had a moment like this in years.

They all let the music of the birds come into them, and Puppet flapped his arms again as if he were flying. Then he took Claude from his pocket and held him high towards the birds and moved him through the air as if he were flying too.

And Antonia caught her breath.

One of the birds dropped and flapped above Puppet as if to catch Claude in its beak. Puppet ran back to the table with his little puppet in his hand.

Antonia caught her breath again and held her hands out, and Puppet put the paper puppet into them, and she whispered, *"Claude!"*

20

They all paused. The garden seemed very still.

"Mum?" said Fleur.

"I *made* him," said Antonia. "I *sent* him."

"You're *that* Antonia?" said Silvester. "You're the Antonia who sent us Claude?"

"Yes." She laughed. "Yes. Yes!"

Fleur reached out and touched the little puppet.

"I told you," Antonia said to her daughter. "Silvester brought his theatre to the riverbank. Afterwards I made a little puppet and posted it to him."

"But you didn't tell me he was called Claude and that he'd come back again!"

Antonia looked down at the puppet in her hand.

"We didn't know, did we?" she said gently. "Hello, Claude. Remember me?"

Fleur ran into the house and came back with a photograph.

"We wanted to show you this," she said to Silvester.

She put it on the table. There was Antonia as a little girl. And there at her side were young Silvester and young Belinda with the open curtains of the puppet theatre just behind them.

"You look just like a younger Fleur!" Silvester said.

Antonia nodded. "I was six years old. It was the tale of Hansel and Gretel."

"Ah, that one!" said Silvester.

"Yes, that one."

Fleur's mum closed her eyes and drifted through time.

"The show was in a tent beside a narrow stream. I can still smell it. The puppets seemed alive. I felt that I was Gretel, going into the dark, dark forest. I was so scared. I held my dad's hand all the way through the performance. I was so relieved when the children got out of the forest again!"

Silvester drifted too. He remembered holding Hansel by his strings. Belinda at his side held Gretel. They moved the puppets step by step by frightening step towards the perilous cottage.

"I knew exactly what was going to happen," he said. "But still it was scary every time, even for me!"

"Afterwards I wanted to tell you how wonderful it was," said Antonia. "But I was too young and shy. I couldn't speak. Dad did, though. He told you it was one of the most beautiful things he'd ever seen."

"How kind of him," Silvester said. He felt so warm inside.

"Then at home, we made puppets from paper and sticks

and card. We made a puppet theatre from a cardboard box and acted out Hansel and Gretel for ourselves. And I made a little puppet named Claude, parcelled him up and took him to the post office and I sent him to you."

"And all these years later," said Silvester, "he fell out of a scrapbook straight into Kenneth's hands."

"Hello again, Claude," said Antonia.

"Hello again, Antonia," she made him say back.

"Jam," said Puppet. "Jam!"

They laughed at the strangeness of it all.

"I think you had to come," said Fleur to Silvester.

"Did we?"

"Yes. We had to meet in the park. You had to come to Crow Hall. You had to bring Kenneth and Claude with you. It's like a story. It's like it couldn't happen any other way."

21

Puppet ran down the garden on the pathways through the trees. Fleur ran with him. The jackdaws flew above and called their jackdaw calls. They flapped above Puppet as if they wanted to swoop down and carry him away.

"No!" yelled Fleur. She wafted her arms at them. "No!"

She shook her fist at them but she was giggling, too.

The birds called as if they were giggling back at her. They danced above her head, flapping their black wings in the empty air.

She took Puppet's hand. "Come on, Kenneth!"

And off they ran, disappearing and appearing behind the trees, moving through shadows and light.

Silvester and Antonia sat at their table, their teacups still in their hands.

"Your garden's like a stage," said Silvester suddenly.

Antonia looked around. "I suppose it is!"

It was so beautiful and true. The trunks of the trees and the low horizontal branches were like the frame. The pathways and the surrounding trees and the wall behind were like scenery. The sun poured down through the foliage like stage lighting. The girl and the puppet ran and walked and danced through the light and the shade, and the birds in the air and on the branches accompanied them with flight and dance and song.

"Like an ancient magical stage," said Silvester softly. "Maybe the first of all stages were like this, long, long ago." He lowered his voice. "Look, Belinda," he whispered.

Yes, came Belinda's voice from the distant past. *It is so lovely, Silvester.*

He sighed. He felt she was so close to him.

"Maybe it was in places like these," he murmured, "that everything began."

22

Fleur picked up a twig and walked it across the grass. Puppet copied her, with another twig.

Fleur spoke with the scratchy voice of a twig. Puppet made scratchy twiggy noises of his own.

Fleur lifted a stone and spoke in the dull heavy voice of a stone. She held it up high and made it sing some nonsense song about being a cold, cold stone and being all, all alone.

She dropped the stone on the grass and Puppet lifted it up and held it towards her and made little stony grunty noises of his own.

"What a weird lovely thing you are!" said Fleur.

She kneeled in front of Puppet and stared and stared at him. It was like she was trying to stare right into him, right past those bright green eyes and into the very heart and soul of him.

Puppet stared back with those bright green eyes.

The sweetest of birds sang in the highest of trees.

"What are you, Kenneth?" whispered Fleur.

She gently touched his head. Puppet reached out and touched her head.

"Are you real?" she wondered.

She touched his three-fingered hand. She touched

his hard head, his hard smooth cheek.

He let Fleur touch him, let her stare into his bright green eyes.

"It *can't* be true," she whispered to Puppet. "Can it, Kenneth?"

"Jam," he said, very softly. "Jam."

Silvester drank his tea and watched his puppet. He watched how Fleur stared and stared. He thought of his work in the attic. He thought of all his work through all the years of his long life. Now his puppet stood in a wild and beautiful garden with a girl named Fleur. He could walk and run and dance and he could call to the birds above his head. How alive he was! How bold and brave!

Silvester laughed. Why not? Why shouldn't Puppet be alive when creatures like jackdaws were alive, when children like Fleur were alive, when even huge things like the trees were alive? Why shouldn't it be possible to make a creature from wood and string and to give it life?

He watched the pair set off again, running, skipping, dancing through the shadows and the light, like any two children, happy together in a beautiful garden.

"Her father passed away," said Antonia softly, suddenly.

"Oh," said Silvester. "I'm so sorry."

"Three years back. We'd just moved here. We were going to work together to bring this place to life."

"You *are* doing that."

"Now we are. But there are times when it has all seemed far too much, when I just wanted to abandon it all."

"But you didn't."

"No. It seemed too important. We nourish the garden, and the garden nourishes us. And so we will go on."

She took a deep, deep breath and smiled.

As if she knew what they were talking about, Fleur turned to them and smiled and waved, then took Puppet's hand again and led him once more through the shadows and the light.

"Look how they run!" said Antonia. "Her dad would have been so proud of her."

"Of course he would."

And here they came, running together back to the table.

Puppet fell with a clatter to the ground, his legs askew. Fleur flopped into a chair.

"How?" she asked.

"How what?" said Silvester.

"You *made* him, didn't you? You brought him to life. I know you did. Please tell me how."

23

"You made him and you brought him to life," Fleur said again.

"Did I?" said Silvester. "How on earth could I do that?" He smiled. There was a twinkle in his eye.

"I don't know. But you did. I know you did."

Antonia watched and listened silently.

"He did, didn't he, Mum?"

"I don't know, Fleur," she said.

"He must have. Nobody realizes, because nobody would think it possible. And Kenneth's got two legs and two arms and a body and a head and so he looks like us and he walks like us, and that's what they see. But if they really *looked*..."

Puppet gazed up at her with his bright green eyes.

"He made you, didn't he?" Fleur said to him.

Puppet stared.

"He did. I know he did."

"You don't think he's a boy?" asked Silvester.

"No. Well, he is, but he's not like other boys. He's a boy and something else."

"Ah, a boy and something else. I am very proud of him." Silvester realized, then, that this was true.

"He's a miracle."

"Not a miracle. The world is the miracle." Silvester

paused. How could he explain it to her? "He's just a puppet that I made in the middle of the night."

"Could I do the same?"

"I don't know, Fleur. I made him one night, but really it took me a whole lifetime."

"I *have* a whole lifetime. I'm only ten. Where do I start? What will I need?"

"Not much at all," said Silvester. "At the beginning, just bits of wood. Something to hold them together. Some string, perhaps. Just a few bits and pieces and odds and ends. And that's about all. Apart from an imagination, and a belief that you can really do it."

24

They cleared the table of the teapot, the milk jug, the cups, the plates and knives.

Fleur went hunting in the garden for twigs and sticks. Puppet ran back and forth by her side. She carried the wood to the table and spread it out. Her mum brought out thread and string from the cottage. She found a small rusty hacksaw, a little hammer and some nails, some cardboard, some sticky tape. There was a box of crayons, a painting set, a tube of glue.

Silvester laughed. "Aha! Proper puppet-making stuff!"

"I'm sure you've got much better tools," said Antonia.

"I have. But they're very simple things. And what really matters is the puppet maker, not the tools."

He ran his fingers over the wood.

"How lovely," he whispered. "A table filled with puppets waiting to be born. A whole *garden* filled with puppets waiting to be born."

The birds in the garden sang. The sun moved through the sky.

Fleur stood at the table. "Shall I start?" she asked.

"Yes," said Silvester. "Of course, we can't really make a puppet like Kenneth today. And, Fleur, *you* won't be able to make a puppet like Kenneth for your first one." He laughed again. "I'm an old man, after all. I've been making puppets for a thousand years."

"A thousand years!" said Fleur.

"Yes! Give or take a year or two. Let's start in simple ways."

He lifted a nicely curved stick. "Isn't this a lovely leg," he said.

"And here's another one," said Fleur.

"Excellent!" said Silvester. "Now find a body and two arms."

She did that. A short stout stick for the body and two twiggy bits for arms.

"What do I do now?"

"You find a way to tie them all together so they're something like a human shape. Doesn't matter if it's messy and dangly. Use that string. Or that thread. Or that sticky tape. It's up to you."

Fleur set to work. She tied string around the top of the first leg and tied it to the body. She did the same with the second leg and the two arms. She held it up and laughed.

"What a mess!" she said.

"A lovely dangly mess," said Silvester. "Now find something that'll make a head."

There was nothing suitable on the table.

"A stone would be too heavy, wouldn't it?" she said. "I know!" She ran off through the trees, and came back with a pine cone. She wove a length of string through the segments of the cone, then tied it to the top of the body.

"What a very weird thing!" she said.

She held it up to show her mum and Silvester.

"Hello," she made it say in a squeaky voice. *"My name is Cone Head."*

"Hello, Cone Head," said her mum. "Welcome to the world."

Cone Head was just the start.

"What next?" Fleur asked Silvester.

"You just make more," he said. "You practise, practise, practise."

So Fleur plunged onwards. Once she'd started, it was like she couldn't stop.

Very quickly, she made a whole clutch of weird little puppets.

It was easy. The basic shape was always the same. Legs, arms, body, head. Twigs, sticks, pine cones, leaves, nuts, feathers, ancient berries, bits of bark. She bound them together with string and thread and glue and sticky tape. For some, she drew faces on bits of paper or card, cut those out and stuck them on. Grinning faces, weepy faces, scary faces. She laid them out on the table; she stood them against the trunks of trees; she hung them from low branches. She made weird puppet animals, things that looked something like dogs or cats or cows or sheep. She made long-armed monkey things and squat hippopotamus things. Lizards and snakes and creatures with wings like swallows or eagles.

So many of them were so quick and easy to make. So many of them needed hardly any work at all.

Looked at in the right way, two simple twigs in a cross shape could look like a boy about to fly or a girl about to dive. A twig with bird feathers stuck to it became an angel or a fairy or a bird.

Silvester watched and smiled and knew the joy that she was experiencing, the joy he'd known as a puppet-making little boy.

"Keep going and keep going and keep going," he said.

"The feel of puppets seeps into your fingers, the images of puppets grow in your mind."

He and Antonia drank more tea and ate more cake.

The number of puppets grew and grew.

"How many shall I make?" asked Fleur.

"A million!" said Silvester.

"A million? I couldn't do that!"

"Couldn't you? Of course you could. Look at that tree!"

"Which tree?"

He pointed to one of the massive oaks. "That tree!"

"What about it?"

"Go and touch it."

She went to it and touched it with the tip of her index finger. She spread her palm across its lovely rough bark. She leaned against it and spread her arms around it.

"Now," said Silvester. "Think how many puppets could be made out of that tree!"

Fleur laughed. The tree was so huge, so wide, so high. Such a massive trunk, such heavy branches twisting towards the sky.

"A million!" she cried.

"Correct! Now touch your head."

"My head?"

"Yes. Touch it."

So she touched her head with the tip of her index finger. It was as hard as the oak tree.

"And now," said Silvester, "think of how many puppets could be imagined in that head!"

She laughed again. "A million!" she said. "A million million!"

"Correct. So make a million more and then we'll think of making something like our Kenneth. Crack on!"

So she cracked on, but after a while she paused.

"We need better ways to hold all the puppets together, don't we? We probably need to drill little holes and carve little slots and make little joints so that the puppets can move about more like humans. And attach the strings properly, and make proper handles for the puppets to dangle from. We do, don't we? We couldn't make something like Kenneth with bits of fallen branches and bits of string."

"No," agreed Silvester, "of course we couldn't. But for now we're probably making puppets like children did thousands of years ago."

Fleur grinned. "Even before you were alive!"

"Yes! Even before I was alive. Crack on. I'll bring some better puppet-making tools next time I come."

"When will that be?"

"Very soon, I hope. And in the meantime, even the clumsiest and most imperfect of puppets has real life in it."

Silvester lifted a dangly arrangement of twigs with an acorn for a tiny head.

"Don't you, Mrs Acorn Head?" he asked.

"I do indeed," Mrs Acorn Head replied.

25

Time moved on. Fleur cracked on. Silvester and Antonia ate sandwiches and cheese and more cakes and they drank tea and lemonade. Fleur grabbed things to quickly eat and drink but she cracked on, cracked on.

The day passed by. Silvester gazed into the garden, this strange stage. There were puppets everywhere. They dangled from branches; they lay on the grass, in the under-growth, among the flowers, against the walls. Some looked like strange new forms of life or like beings from other worlds. Some blended with the fallen branches that they came from. Some were already falling apart, coming loose from their strings. Legs and arms had become detached. Heads had dropped. Some puppets had become sticks and fallen twigs again.

The sturdiest survived, and looked as if they could start to move, to walk. Puppet wandered among these new cousins of his. He inspected them. He lifted some up and held them as if they might walk like he did. He turned his ear to them, as if they were about to break into speech or song. He whispered his own words into their little wooden ears.

"Jak! Jam! Hell-o."

Light started falling. Darkness was coming on. Shadows under the trees deepened. The sky reddened beyond the trees and above the garden wall.

Silvester suddenly felt tired.

"We should go soon," he said to Antonia.

"Shall we do a show before you leave?" suggested Fleur. "We could all join in."

"All of us?" said Silvester.

"Yes! We'll make a show of puppets and people all together."

Her face was shining, pale like the moon.

"Please," she said. "Just a little one."

How could he refuse?

"I'll make masks for the humans!" she said.

She quickly scribbled faces onto pieces of card big enough to cover human heads. Made bands from string and card to go around the heads. She poked in eyeholes. She gave two masks to Silvester and Antonia and took one for herself.

"Put the masks on," she ordered. "Turn into puppet people. And you, Kenneth," she said to Puppet. "Should you have a mask too so that *you* can pretend to be a puppet?"

"Jam!"

She laughed. "Maybe not."

Fleur's mum switched on the lamps in the cottage, and shafts of light shone into the garden through the windows and the open door. A bright crescent moon rose over the roof and shone down onto the wilderness.

Silvester, Antonia and Fleur moved deeper into the garden, into the shadows beneath the trees.

"How do we begin, puppet master?" Fleur asked Silvester.

He smiled at her. "This show is yours. What story shall we do?"

Fleur pondered. "How about a simple story that we can all just make up as we go along?"

"What's its name?" said Silvester.

She pondered some more. "Ah! It's called *The Day We Created Puppets in the Ancient Garden*."

"An excellent title!" said Silvester.

"The performance is very free-form," Fleur added.

Silvester laughed. "Have you got a trumpet? Belinda and I would always blow a trumpet before we performed."

Fleur frowned.

"It calls the audience," Silvester explained. "It wakes everybody up. We used to say it woke the puppets up, too."

She shook her head. "I don't think we have," she said.

"Never mind. I've got an old one somewhere. And for today…"

126

He cupped his hands together in a trumpet shape. He leaned back and took a deep breath and called and hooted through his hands.

"*Da-da-da-da, da-da-da-da. Doot-doot-doot-doot. Whoop whoop whoop whoop!*"

He ran out of breath. He coughed and coughed. He laughed and laughed.

"Now you," he said.

And Fleur did the same, and tooted trumpet noises into the garden.

And then Antonia did the same.

And Puppet watched and lifted his face to the sky as if he was trumpeting too.

"*Jam jam jam jam!*"

"What a lovely weird noise," Silvester said. He put his finger to his lips. "Now *shh*," he whispered. "Everything is woken. Belinda used to say the trumpets even woke the dead."

They were all very quiet, very still.

"Lovely," murmured Silvester. "Everything's prepared. Now let's begin."

And they began. They moved through the garden, beneath the trees, on the curving pathways. Antonia and even Silvester were a little shy and awkward at first, but soon they became as free as Fleur and Puppet, who skipped and danced and twirled. They lifted up puppets and held them and moved them as if they were alive. Humans and puppets swayed, shifted, danced.

"We should give ourselves new names," said Fleur. "We should become different beings and truly act our parts." She laughed. "I am now … Esperenza."

She turned away from the others and moved her body in new, Esperenza-ish ways. She spoke with a new Esperenza-ish voice.

"My name is Quetzalcoatl," muttered Silvester to himself.

"Suzanna Chesterfield," whispered Antonia.

"Jam!" said Puppet.

They moved and murmured as these new beings. They gave names to the puppets they held.

The garden was filled with whispers, murmurings, cries and laughter. In the gathering dark, it wasn't clear who or what made these noises. It was never certain whether a grunt or a squeak was a word or a song or an outburst of pain or joy. It was not clear whether the noises came from human mouths or from the mouths of puppets. It was not certain who was a puppet and who was not. Who was living or who was not.

Did Silvester, Antonia, Puppet and Fleur even exist at all?

An owl hooted somewhere above. Bats flickered in the moonlight. A dark cat, and another cat, very pale. Little mice and other tiny scurrying creatures. And was that a rabbit, that a rat?

And was that a fox back there against the garden wall, its eyes shining where they caught the light?

Look deeper, deeper into the dark towards the shifting shadows, shifting shapes.

Is this when the wolves begin to appear?

Is this when strange shapes turn to monsters?

Is this when darkness takes the physical forms that haunt the ancient tales?

Were the minotaurs, the dragons and the ghouls about to come?

Were those fairies dancing there in the moonbeams, and was that an angel glowing in the sky?

The humans and the puppets danced through the garden, across this strange and beautiful and scary stage.

And then, as if they'd all been called, they gathered together under the long thick horizontal branch of the great oak tree.

A late bird – a nightingale? – still sang in the highest foliage.

Slowly the humans came back to themselves. They left behind their new names and identities. They took off their masks. They came back into the real world – if this truly is the world that is real.

They looked at each other wide-eyed, as if seeing one another for the very first time.

"I'll remember for ever and for ever," whispered Fleur.

"Yes," said Silvester.

"Yes," echoed Antonia.

Silvester yawned. "I'm very tired now," he said.

"A final cup of tea?" suggested Fleur's mum.

Silvester and Antonia sat at the table and drank more tea.

Fleur and Puppet stayed out there on the garden stage. They sat back to back, unspeaking – like old friends, like siblings.

When at last Silvester stood up to leave, Fleur said, "We should put on a proper puppet show, Silvester."

"Should we?"

"Yes. With an audience. And with a stage, and a poster, and…"

Silvester smiled. "Perhaps we should. I thought I'd finished with all that. But maybe I can never be finished until… You've given me new life, Fleur. Just like Puppet's given me new life. How strange," he said. "How very unexpected."

"Now let Silvester and Kenneth go, love," said Antonia. "It's been quite a day for them."

Silvester yawned again. "I could sleep for an age," he said.

They all hauled open the heavy gate.

Silvester and Puppet squeezed through and helped to slide it shut again.

"Goodnight," they cried to one another. "Goodnight. Goodnight. Goodnight."

26

Silvester and Puppet made their way homewards beneath the crescent moon.

It was as if they'd been in another dimension, in another world. The edges of the hills beyond the rooftops were dark and sharp against the moonlit sky.

A shooting star fell. And another.

"Did you see?" said Silvester.

Puppet turned to him. There was no way to know.

Hand in hand they walked through the little estate. The night was warm, the air was still. A guitar still played. Perhaps Malcolm's ghost would soon appear.

"The dog!" called a woman's voice. "That silly dog again!"

Silvester kept looking up at the night above. So many stars, star after star after glittering star. He lifted Puppet up and turned his face towards them.

"What do you see?" Silvester asked.

Puppet was silent. Not even a "Jam!" came from his lips.

"There are a million million million stars," Silvester told him. "There are worlds that stretch for ever and for ever." Think of the millions of puppets that might exist out there."

Puppet held Claude up to see too.

Silvester laughed and carefully lowered Puppet. Puppet

stood for a moment at Silvester's side, then he fell with a little clatter to the pavement.

"Puppet," cried Silvester. "Puppet!"

No answer. Puppet was hard and cold and silent and still, lying all askew upon the ground.

Silvester lifted him up, tucked Claude into his pocket, and carried him gently onwards. In the square, there were people inside Dragone's and sitting at the outside tables. Candles were burning. A woman somewhere sang sweetly about dreams and love.

"Hello, Silvester."

It was Louis, the coffee-drinking, card-playing man. He was sitting with a woman, holding her hand.

"My wife," he said. "Christine. Would you like to join us for a glass of wine?" Then he saw Puppet in Silvester's arms. "Perhaps not. All worn out, I see."

Christine leaned over to take a look. "He's so sweet," she softly said.

"He is."

"Good night," they called as Silvester headed off.

On he walked. On down the lane and into the house.

"Are you simply sleeping, Puppet," Silvester said, "or have you gone?"

He laid Puppet down, this beautiful, imperfect arrangement of wood and string, of paint and love.

"Night-night," he whispered, and he did not know if

this puppet would ever wake again.

He sighed happily, he yawned deeply, and he went to his own bed and tumbled into it as Puppet had tumbled to the pavement.

Silvester entered the deepest, deepest, deepest sleep.

He dreamed that he was underground, deep down in the soil. It was so warm, so comfortable down there.

And he dreamed that an oak tree grew up from the soil around him. It started as a tiny acorn. Pale tender tiny roots grew downward. Then pale tender tiny shoots grew up and out into the air. They strengthened, thickened, turned to trunk, branches, twigs and dark green leaves.

The oak tree grew into the world above Silvester. It became a massive living lovely thing that reached for the sun and for the sky.

And Silvester dreamed of puppet after puppet walking out from the trunk of that great oak tree. He smiled to see them go: girls and boys and dogs and cats and men and women, snakes and birds, frogs and tigers, dragons and beasts. There they went, one by one, score by score, a never-ending stream, stepping out from the great tree onto the earth and into the sky.

☆ ☆ ☆

In her own home, in her own bed, Fleur also dreamed.

Her dream was of the puppets that grew from deep

135

inside her body and her mind. They started off as tiny dots of life. They grew, and moved out onto her pillow. They slipped away into the night, into the world.

In her sleep, she laughed to see them leave.

And over all of it, the owls hooted, the bats flitted, the moon slid through the sky, and the sun rose and fell and the moon moved through the dark, and the sun rose and fell and rose again and time did pass

did pass

did pass

did pass.

27

Knock-knock! Knock-knock!

Puppet kicked and kicked against the bedpost. Nothing happened. He kicked again.

Whack-whack! Whack-whack!

Silvester didn't stir.

"Jam, jam! Jam, jam! Jak jak! Jam, jam!"

Knock-knock! Knock-knock! Whack-whack!

Puppet swung his leg and kicked harder. His body rattled. The bed trembled.

WHACK-WHACK! WHACK-WHACK!

He called louder. "JAM JAM! *JAK JAK!*"

He poked Silvester on the shoulder. He tapped Silvester's head.

At last, Silvester stirred. It was like coming up from such a long way down. Like coming back from so much deepest, deepest dark. Like coming back to being Silvester again after being nobody at all.

Silvester opened his eyes. He closed them again. The sun was so bright.

WHACK-WHACK! WHACK-WHACK!

"All right, Puppet," he muttered. "No need to—"

WHACK-WHACK!

"No need to kick, Puppet."

WHACK-WH—

Silvester reached out from under the covers and grabbed Puppet's leg and stilled it. He glanced at the clock on the wall.

"Look at the time! Afternoon already, Puppet! Where have we been?"

Silvester tried to sit up. He groaned. "So stiff," he said. "So sore."

He did sit up. Swung his legs from beneath the covers, sat at the edge of the bed. Sore back, sore legs, sore neck.

"Aaahhh," he mumbled. He rubbed his joints. "Come on, old bones."

Tried to stand, sat again, stood again, sat again. Teetered on the floor like a thing about to fall. Lay back down on the bed again. Rubbed his knees.

"Aaahhh. My legs are turning to timber, Puppet. My bones are turning to wood. I'm turning into a puppet, Puppet!"

He tried to rub life and warmth into himself, and sighed when Puppet reached out with his three-fingered hand and tried to rub tenderly too, and looked down at his puppet master and gently went, "Ah. Aaahhh. Aaahhh."

"Aaahhh," said Silvester back. "Thank you, Puppet. That's lovely, my Puppet." There were tears in his eyes. "What a good lad you are," he softly said.

He gazed into his puppet's bright green lovely eyes. "I need some more kip, son."

"Jam."

"Yes." Silvester nodded. "Go and get yourself some jam."

"Jam!"

"Silvester's tired," said Silvester. "You can look after yourself for an hour or two."

He sighed. How on earth could Puppet understand?

"Be a good boy," he whispered. "I'll be right as rain in a little while."

And he closed his eyes again, pulled the covers over himself once more, and drifted back to sleep.

28

Puppet stood by Silvester's bed with his arms dangling at his side and his head slumped forward.

"E-O," he said.

Silvester snored on.

Puppet took Claude from his pocket and stared at him.

"E-O," he said again.

No answer.

He went downstairs and looked up at the picture of Belinda.

"E-O."

No answer.

He went into the kitchen and opened a cupboard and took out a jar of raspberry jam.

"E-O," he said. "Jam. Mmm."

He managed to unscrew the lid. He dipped his three-fingered hand in and smeared jam across his mouth.

"Jam!" he said loudly. "Mmm! Mmmmm!"

He took more jam, and more again. He smeared it across

his mouth. He wiped his fingers on the worktop.

"Mmm!" he said. "Mmmmm."

He stopped. He went to the window and clambered up onto the sill. He leaned against the glass and stared out. Sunlight poured down into the lane. He turned his head. Children's voices came from far away.

He climbed down. He went to the bottom of the stairs and looked up.

Nothing.

"E-O!" he said. "E-O!"

He wandered through the rooms and his limbs click-clacked, click-clacked.

He practised moving fast and slow. He practised swinging his arms and swinging his legs.

He gave a little skip, a little jump. He did a little jiggly dance.

He stood very, very still.

He looked at the front door. He looked away. He looked again.

He went to the door and reached up to the handle and turned it.

And he pushed, and the door opened, and the outside air rushed in.

He leaned forward across the threshold.

And out he stepped, and the door swung shut behind him.

29

Puppet stepped out and walked along the lane. His limbs softly rattled. His feet click-clacked. He swung his arms. He turned his face towards the sun.

He came to the end of the lane and he paused. There was the big wide world spread out before him. There were the distant voices of children.

He tottered into the square. Louis and his friends were sitting at their table.

"Hello, Kenneth!" Louis called. "All on your own today?"

Puppet didn't turn. He just kept on walking.

A couple of jackdaws fluttered over him and fluttered away again.

"Jak jak!" they called.

Puppet kept on. He swung his arms. He swung his legs. He was dapper little Puppet walking on his own through the square.

He passed the busker, who was playing his guitar by the fountain. Puppet did a little dance and carried on. He walked faster, then stumbled. He stumbled again and fell. He pulled himself back up and set off again.

Puppet hurried on. He passed the butcher's shop and the butcher glared from inside.

Puppet became a little jerkier. A big brown dog ran at him and barked and bared its teeth. Puppet swung his leg and tried to kick but he missed. The dog snarled. Somebody yelled and the dog gave another snarl and ran back to them.

Puppet looked around, as if searching for Silvester. He lifted his hand, as if he expected Silvester to take it in his.

He hurried on.

The sun was very bright. The sky was huge. The square was huge. The traffic rumbled. Children yelled. Puppet limped and jerked.

"Jam!" he said. "Jam, jam!"

Where was he going?

He began to totter in circles across the grass. Some big boys saw him and they pointed and laughed. One of them imitated Puppet's walk and they all roared and roared before they ran away, still laughing.

"Are you all right, little boy?" an old lady asked him. "They're just big daft brutes."

"Jam," said Puppet.

"Jam? I don't have any with me, I'm afraid."

She came a little closer. Puppet watched her with his bright green shining eyes.

"Where's your mummy?" she asked. "I'm sure she can't be far away. Shall I call for her?" She looked around, wondering where Puppet's mum could be. "Where do you live?" she said. "Can I take you home?"

She reached out her hand to him. "What's your name? I'm Maddy Blenkinsop."

Puppet just stared at her.

Laurence from Cakes of Heaven was heading across the square with a plate of cakes in one hand. He was waving. The man called Louis was coming too. Lisette was at her door with a pair of scissors shining in her hand. The butcher stood with his arms folded outside his meaty window, glaring.

Somebody called Puppet's name. "Kenneth! Kenneth!"

Puppet tottered away from Maddy.

Here came the big brown dog again and its owner yelling, "Buster! No!"

Buster ran at Puppet, snarling, then ran away again.

"Don't be scared," said Maddy.

Puppet swung his leg and tried to kick her. She flinched.

"No!" she protested, shocked. "Don't do that!"

Puppet panicked, turned, tottered, stumbled, ran again.

He ran towards the road, towards the park, head flung back, arms swinging. Now the big boys were there with their silly mocking and their silly laughs. Puppet picked up frantic speed. Here came that big brown dog again. Puppet came to the road, to the crossing. There was the park, just beyond. There were some people ready to cross.

"Wait for the green man!" somebody yelled.

Puppet didn't wait. He ran into the road. And here came a gleaming silver car, very fast.

30

There was a squeal of brakes, then the sound of screaming. Everything stopped. A moment of dead stillness. Dead silence. Then people gathered on the pavement; dared to step into the road. Here came Louis and Laurence and Lisette and all those who had been waiting for the green man. Here came people out of the park. Here were Tom and his mum.

Frightened onlookers, hands across their mouths, hands over their eyes. Screams and gasps and horrified whispers.

Oh, and there was little Puppet lying in the road with the bumper of the silver car over his head, and the front wheel right beside his chest.

And here was the ashen-faced driver getting out of his car. A young man, in jeans and a flowery shirt.

"He just ran out!" he gasped. "I'm sure I didn't hit him!"

He crouched beside Puppet.

"I'm sure I didn't," he said again. "I'm sure I just missed! I'm so sorry," he sobbed.

The crowd inched closer.

"Give him space!" someone yelled.

"Is he dead?" yelled someone else.

Puppet moved. He shifted one leg, then another. The driver reached out.

"Let him lie there, mate!" someone called. "Give him time!"

Puppet sat up. He stared at the faces around him.

"Call an ambulance!"

Puppet squirmed on the tarmac, untangled his limbs.

"No! No need for that! He's fine!"

It was Fleur, weaving her way through the bodies.

"Let me through," she said.

They tried to hold her back. She kept on coming.

"I'm his sister!" she said quickly. "Kenneth! It's me! It's Fleur!"

She hurried towards him. Puppet tottered to his feet and held out his arms.

"Jam!" he called. "Jam, jam!"

She patted him on the shoulder, then turned her head and called, "He's fine, Mum! He's safe! Mum!"

"I'm coming!" Antonia called back. And here she came, twisting her way through the crowd.

She lifted Puppet into her arms.

"Yes, he's fine," she said, relieved. "But what a nasty fright!" She touched the driver's arm. "Are you all right?" she asked.

The driver was crying. "He just ran out!" he said. "I'm so sorry."

"We know. But he's fine. Aren't you, Kenneth?"

"Jam."

"See," said Antonia. "Not a scratch on him."

"Are you sure?" said the driver.

"Yes. Come along, son. We'll get you home."

She moved towards the square, holding Puppet. Fleur followed. The bodies parted.

"You have to wait for the green man, Kenneth," said Fleur. "How many times have we told you?"

At the centre of the square, they paused.

"What on earth were you doing out here all alone?" whispered Fleur.

No answer, of course.

"Where is Silvester?" she asked.

The big boys came over. "We're really sorry," said the biggest. "We didn't mean to frighten him."

And Maddy Blenkinsop. "He did seem rather agitated," she said.

"He just ran off," said Fleur's mum. "He does that sometimes."

"Like my little laddie used to do," said Maddy. "Lads, eh?"

They moved on.

Laurence came over, carrying a jam tart.

"This'll sort him out," he said. He gave it to Antonia, bowed, then went back to his shop.

"What was he doing out here all alone?" said Fleur again.

"And where on earth is Silvester?" said Antonia.

Fleur and her mother looked at each other in dismay. They realized they didn't know the way to go.

Then Louis was at their side.

"It didn't seem right," he said. "Little Kenneth all alone, and no Silvester by his side."

"You haven't seen Silvester?" asked Antonia.

"Not these past few days." He pointed to the lane. "Go along there. It's the door at the very far end."

Into the lane they walked. They came to the door. They knocked.

No answer.

They knocked again.

"Silvester!" called Fleur through the letterbox. "Silvester!"

Then the door opened and the puppet master was there, rubbing sleep from his eyes.

"Antonia," he said. "And Fleur! What a— Puppet! What are you doing out there on your own?"

31

They all went into the house. Fleur and her mum told Silvester the scary tale. He was aghast.

"I should have been with you, Puppet," he said. "It could have been the end of you, my little one!"

He sat on the sofa holding Puppet close.

"I just couldn't wake up," he told them.

He stared at Puppet.

"I said you could look after yourself for a little while. I didn't mean go outside all alone! Just imagine. If Antonia and Fleur had not been there... What would have..."

He turned to Fleur.

"How was it that you *were* there?"

"We were so worried," said Fleur.

"So worried?"

"We hadn't heard from you for days," said Antonia. "We thought something must have happened."

"As you see," Silvester said, "I'm perfectly fine. And so, no thanks to me, is Puppet."

"I began to think it was all a dream," said Fleur. "I started to think you hadn't been to see us at all."

"What a very odd notion," said Silvester.

He tapped Puppet on the head. "This one doesn't seem

too dreamlike." He tapped his own head. "And nor do I. Shall I put the kettle on?"

"But where *have* you been?" asked Fleur.

"Fleur," said her mum. "That's none of our business."

"Where have I been?" said Silvester. "Just here at home, of course, and fast asleep and…"

He frowned, and took a deep breath. "What day is it?" he asked.

"It's Saturday," said Antonia.

"Saturday?"

"Yes."

"But that means…" He counted on his fingers. "That means, Puppet, that I've been asleep for three whole days!"

"Jam!" said Puppet.

"Jam indeed! No wonder I took some waking up. It was like coming back from…" Silvester put his hand across his mouth. "Three whole days! I'd better get some toast inside me."

He paused and shook his head.

"I've never slept for three whole days in my life! Shall we have tea and toast?"

"Sit still," said Antonia. "You've had quite a shock. I'll make some for us all."

32

"What lovely posters," said Fleur.

She was looking at the gorgeous posters on the walls.

"Thank you," said Silvester. "We were very proud of them."

"And what lovely photographs."

"Thank you again. You can see how happy we were. How lovely we were. Look, there's my beautiful Belinda."

Fleur went to stand in front of Belinda's picture.

"Hello, beautiful Belinda," she said softly.

"Hello, Fleur," said Silvester in a Belinda-ish voice.

They all laughed.

"She would have liked you very much," he said.

"Did you have children?" asked Fleur.

"Ah. No."

"That's a shame."

"Oh, not really. We passed the puppets and the stories on to all the children who came to see us."

He poured some tea, then he got the scrapbooks and notebooks out to show her.

Fleur looked through them with her mum. They smiled and sighed to see the world that had gone before.

"When we make our show, we'll have posters like those, and we'll take photographs like these," decided Fleur.

Silvester laughed. "Oh, we need to start much simpler than that!"

He flicked through one of the scrapbooks and came to a crinkled poster from long, long ago. It was written and drawn with brightly coloured crayons. It said:

SiLveSTAs maJiC PupITS
The beSt yooL EvA see!
Evry saridday at 10 oClok

Below it was a drawing of a boy with a grinning puppet dangling from his hand.

"That's me, little Silvester," said Silvester. "And that's Cod."

"Cod?"

"My first ever puppet with strings. Cod. How I loved him!"

"And you really did a show every Saturday?"

"Well, maybe not *every* Saturday. And just for my mam. Me and Cod and a few more. She loved it!"

"Where's Cod now?"

"Ah, he fell to bits. I put him together again and he kept falling to bits, and I kept putting him together and he kept falling to bits, and in the end I just used parts of him in other puppets that I made." He laughed. "It was almost as if that was what he had wanted all along!"

"So he's in lots of places," said Fleur with a laugh.

"Yes. He's everywhere! Bits of him will be in some of the puppets in the museum. Some bits will be…"

He paused and frowned and pondered, and he looked closely at Puppet.

"Maybe bits of him are even in Kenneth?" Antonia suggested.

"Hmm," said Silvester. "How could *that* be?" Then he closed the book.

"Why Cod?" asked Fleur.

"Eh?"

"Why did you call him Cod?"

"Oh. I liked fish fingers."

Silvester laughed again as it all came back to him.

"One of his friends was called Brown Sauce. Another was called Chips. And another one was Nice Cup of Tea. That was Mam's favourite!"

"And where are they now?" asked Antonia.

"Hahaha! Everywhere too."

Fleur looked around the room. "Is this where you make the puppets?" she asked. "Is this where you made Kenneth?"

"No. I made him up there," said Silvester, pointing to the steep stairway to the attic.

Fleur looked to where he pointed. "Would it be possible to see?"

33

Together, Silvester and Fleur climbed the steep stairs. Fleur carried Puppet in her arms.

Light shone down through the window to the sky. Dust shimmered and swirled and danced in it.

Silvester sat at his workbench and switched on the lamp. Fleur stood beside him, wide-eyed. She saw the bits of puppet lying in the dust, the box of half-made legs and half-made arms, half-carved hands, misshapen feet, the unfinished heads that dangled from the ceiling, the bits of wood that had turned to nothing yet, the tubes of paint and pots of glue, the tweezers, needles, sheets of sandpaper, tiny saws, the box full of clothes, and curls of wire and lengths of string.

Just bits and pieces, fragments, things left behind from the times before, things to create the times to come.

She held Puppet tight.

"This is your birthplace, Puppet," she whispered. "This is where you began."

Silvester laughed.

Woodlice moved across the bench.

Now came the spiders, dangling on their strings.

"Hello, spiders," he said. "Hello, woodlice."

Down by the skirting board, the little mouse squeaked.

"Hello, mouse," said Fleur. "Hello, pigeon," she said to the pigeon at the window to the sky.

She let a spider crawl across her hand. Smiled at the little tickling it made.

"Oh," she whispered. "It's all so beautiful!"

"I'm pleased you think so," Silvester said. "I do too. Pass Puppet to me now."

Fleur handed Puppet over.

"Forgive me for a moment," said Silvester gently to his puppet. "Look closely, Fleur."

And he showed her.

He showed her the joints and the connections that held Puppet together. He showed her where he had to saw, where he had to sand. He showed her the tiny holes that he drilled, the slots that he cut. He showed her where the needle threaded the wires, how the head was fixed to the body. He showed how he sanded and waxed the skin of Puppet's face, how he brightened the eyes, how he attached the hair. He showed how he tightened everything, how he smoothed so much, how he made Puppet the best puppet that he could possibly be.

"And he came to life," said Fleur in wonder.

"Yes. He started to stand on his own. He started to walk. He started to talk. Didn't you, Puppet?"

"Jam," said Puppet.

"But how?" asked Fleur. "*How* did he come to life?"

"I don't really know. It happened as I was holding him, as I was forming him."

"What did you think? What did you do?"

"I thought about all the puppets that there'd ever been. And then I forgot about everything and I thought just about him. I watched him, there in my hands. I was the one who was making him, but it was like he had come to me. Like he had come to the attic from somewhere else. And like he had chosen me, Silvester, to be his maker. "

"Were you frightened?"

"Yes. I wondered if I should stop. But I didn't. I couldn't. I told myself to be brave, to let it happen, to let Puppet be created."

Silvester looked at his own hands now holding Puppet and he shook his head and laughed.

"You're a mystery, aren't you, Puppet? But isn't everything a mystery? Not just you, but every single thing that exists."

"Jam!"

"Yes. Jam."

"Lovely Kenneth," said Fleur. "Beautiful Puppet."

"Yes," said Silvester, "and imperfect too, as the most beautiful things are."

He held him up in the air above the bench.

"He's the puppet that he was destined to be," he said.

The mouse squeaked. The birds sang. Fleur and Silvester smiled.

"And all of this could be yours," said Silvester suddenly.

He surprised himself. He hadn't expected to say such a thing, but now that he had he was very pleased.

"All of what?" Fleur said.

"All of these bits and pieces and all of these tools. These ancient bits of puppet. This bench, this chair, this attic. They're yours to use, Fleur. If you'd like to have them, of course. You don't have to. It's all up to you."

She smiled. All up to her. Yes, maybe this was how it should be. It was like being in a story again, but in a story that was true.

Already she had a vision of puppets coming to life between her hands as she sat at this bench.

Silvester stood up. He adjusted the chair so that the seat was higher.

Fleur took his place.

She ran her hand through a box full of puppet clothes.

She picked up a tiny saw, a pair of tweezers.

She lifted up a tiny wooden foot.

It was like it had all been waiting for her.

"You'll know how to use them," said Silvester. "You'll know how to bring the fragments to life."

He moved away from the workbench.

"Start now if you'd like to," he said. "Create what you will."

And down he went again, and left Fleur there with Puppet and her dreams.

34

At first Fleur just messed about. She played with the tools. She slid the saw across her skin to feel the roughness of it, touched a needle point to her palm to feel it so sharp. Peered into the eyes of puppet heads. Laid out arms and legs and torsos, arranged them in patterns on the bench top, reshaped, rearranged. Unravelled lengths of wool and string. Ran her fingers through the dust at the back of the bench. Let spiders and woodlice scuttle around her. Listened to the pigeon and the mouse; sometimes caught the sounds of Silvester and her mother talking downstairs.

Puppet sat on the bench before her, kicking his heels, watching as she touched, weighed, inspected, dreamed. The spiders dangled closer.

Her mind grew stiller, stiller. She remembered the rough and lovely puppets that she'd made in the garden those few short days ago. Had a sudden vision of herself in years to come, sitting here with the bench cleaned and polished and renewed, light shining down from the window. In the vision, there were boxes of new timber before her, collections of bright shiny tools. She was surrounded by many of the puppets that she must have made – lovely things with neat limbs, smooth faces, dressed in bright new clothes. There was a poster on the wall.

FLEUR'S MAGICAL PUPPET THEATRE

She turned her mind back to the present again, to being here in this lovely old place.

She breathed, breathed.

She lifted an awkwardly shaped arm.

"I'll start with you," she whispered.

Puppet watched closely.

She lifted another arm.

"And with you," she said.

And she started connecting piece with piece.

35

What is time? How does it pass? Sometimes – maybe when we're bored or when we're waiting for something we really want to do – an hour can seem like a week. Sometimes an hour can seem like a few fleeting moments. And there are times when you forget everything and time doesn't seem to pass at all – like when you're lost in a game, or reading a good book or watching the best TV, or messing about with your favourite friend. That's what the afternoon was like for Fleur. Once she started to create her new puppet, she almost forgot who she was, where she was, what she was doing. It was like she was asleep, or like the world was a dream.

She was engrossed by the thing being formed by her hands.

But time did pass

did pass

did pass.

And when Fleur looked up at last, looked beyond her hands, beyond the bench, beyond the light of the lamp on the bench, the day had faded. Light through the window had diminished. Dusk was coming on.

In her hands she held a puppet.

A girl with mismatched arms and legs, black woollen hair, one green eye and one brown, her mouth turned up in the shape of a smile. A far from perfect but very happy-looking puppet girl, held together with wire and string, and dressed in blue and gold.

Fleur looked down at her. "Hello," she softly said.

Puppet was looking at this new puppet too.

"I'll call you Rosa," Fleur said.

"Hello," she made Rosa say.

She held Rosa towards Puppet and stood her up on the bench at Puppet's side.

"Kenneth," she said. "This is Rosa."

Puppet leaned down, for Rosa was a little shorter than he was.

"Hello, Kenneth," she made Rosa say.

He peered into Rosa's mismatched eyes. He reached out and touched her hand with his.

"Hello, Kenneth," Fleur made Rosa say again.

"E-O," said Puppet.

Fleur laughed. "Well done, Kenneth."

She held Rosa in one arm, took Puppet's hand, and together they climbed down the steep stairway to her mum and Silvester.

36

Of course, they thought that Rosa was beautiful. Silvester said that Fleur would become the finest of puppet makers. Antonia was so pleased and proud.

Fleur held Rosa up on the low table in the living room. She took her hands away and Rosa tumbled. She held her again and swung Rosa's legs as if she was walking, as if she was dancing. She walked her across the floor, Puppet click-clacking at her side. Fleur took her hands away and Rosa fell. Of course she did. What else could she do?

Fleur clicked her tongue. "How can I make her stand like Puppet does?" she asked Silvester.

She stood Rosa up again, and Rosa fell again.

"You need strings, of course," said Silvester. "She has to be controlled by strings. How else can she stand and move?"

He said he would help her.

He climbed to the attic to get some tools and came back down again.

He took a tiny sharp hook and pressed it to the back of Rosa's left hand. He twisted it, and the point went down into Rosa's hand. Fleur gasped, couldn't look. She knew it couldn't be hurting little Rosa, but she also feared that it must be. She could almost feel the tiny sharp hook piercing her own skin.

As Silvester did the same with Rosa's right hand, again Fleur couldn't look.

She peeped as he threaded strings through the hooks. Then he screwed tiny hooks into Rosa's knees and threaded strings through them, too.

Fleur almost let out a scream when Silvester screwed a tiny hook right into the top of Rosa's head. Lastly he threaded a string through that.

He looked up and smiled. Fleur sighed. She felt like she'd been in some great fight.

"All done," said Silvester. "You can look now. Are you OK?"

"Yes," she said. Antonia took her hand.

Silvester had a cross-shaped piece of wood. He tied the ends of the strings to that. He lifted it up and Rosa dangled down.

"And now," he said. "You simply move the cross and the puppet moves."

He showed Fleur how to do it, then handed the puppet back.

She copied him, and relaxed. She started to learn how to move each arm, each leg, how to make the puppet seem to walk and dance again.

All the while, Puppet stayed beside her. Every now and then, he leaned down to peer into Rosa's face.

The strings kept getting tangled. Rosa's limbs got tangled. Fleur disentangled them and started again.

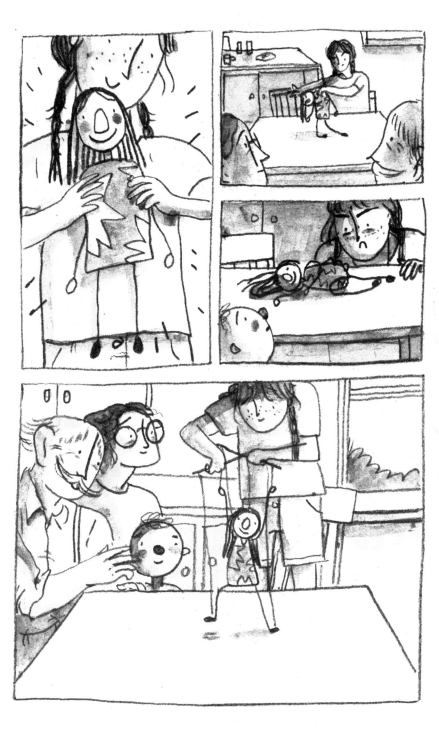

"You'll get better at it," her mum said.

"You'll get better fast," Silvester promised. "And you'll keep on getting better all your life. But lovely Rosa is your first true puppet, and you'll remember her for evermore."

"Like Cod!" said Fleur.

"Yes. And probably she'll keep falling to bits like Cod did. And you'll keep putting her back together again. Look, is that left leg loosening already?"

Yes, it was. Fleur tightened the string holding the left leg.

"That's how it is with your first puppets," said Silvester. "Keeping an eye on them. Tightening and loosening. Keeping them together." He shrugged. "It's all part of the puppeteer's life."

Fleur checked the other strings and attachments. She sighed and smiled.

"It's a lovely thing to do, isn't it?" she said.

"Yes. It is," Silvester agreed. "It's like love," he added softly.

Fleur practised and practised. She checked and tightened.

Soon Antonia said it was almost time to leave. They had presumed on Silvester enough!

"A bit longer, Mum?" said Fleur. "Please?"

Antonia looked at Silvester.

"Yes. Of course," he said.

So Antonia and Silvester sat drinking tea while Fleur and the puppets played together on the floor.

Silvester looked at Belinda on the wall. It might have been like this, he thought, if we'd had a child.

Fleur whispered encouragement to Rosa and moved her elegantly across the carpet.

Then she said to Silvester, "So when shall we do it? When shall we perform the show?"

"Best not beat about the bush," he replied. "Sooner rather than later." He pondered. "Saturday? A week today?"

He blinked. He hadn't expected to say such a thing. A week today!

"Yes!" said Fleur. "That's quite enough time to get everything prepared."

"Wonderful!"

"It's so exciting! And *where* will we do it?"

"Somewhere ordinary," Silvester said. "Somewhere easy. Somewhere near by."

"The town square?" suggested Fleur.

"Yes! That's where Belinda and I did some of our very first shows. Ha! They were very haphazard things. And very lovely things! As ours will be."

"What story shall we do?" she asked him.

"Something easy and ordinary as well."

"Two children go into the forest and come back out again…" began Fleur.

"Aye! That's how so many stories start!"

"I'll get going on the poster." She stared into space for

a moment. "And I'll start making a stage, shall I?" She could already see the show taking place in her mind. "And the scenery," she added.

Silvester laughed. "I suppose we will need something like a stage and some scenery. But nothing fancy. Something makeshift. Something you can lift and carry about with ease."

"We can do that!" cried Fleur.

"Of course you can!" said Antonia.

Silvester laughed again. "You're just like I was, Fleur. You think anything's possible, don't you?"

"Yes! You say you're going to do something, and you get on and do it!"

"Ha ha. Get on and do it," said Silvester. "That's what Belinda and I did at the very start. No messing about, no shillyshallying!"

"We'll meet up in the square," said Fleur. "Set the stage up, send the children off into the forest and bring them back again, and there we are!"

"Excellent. Saturday afternoon!"

"Two o'clock?"

"Two o'clock!"

"And what about the trumpet?" asked Fleur.

"Oh yes. I'm sure I've got one somewhere."

And then Antonia and Fleur did leave. They said goodnight to Silvester and to Puppet, and Fleur's mum thanked Silvester for everything.

"See you on Saturday," she said.

"I won't sleep so long next Saturday," promised Silvester. "I'll wake up in time."

Antonia smiled. "You must sleep as long as you wish," she said.

"No," whispered Silvester. "Not yet."

Fleur and her mum walked from the ancient almost-forgotten lane towards the square and the warmly lit cafes.

Fleur looked at the beautiful ordinary space. A few benches, some trees, the old fountain. A single street light at the centre. People sitting around and strolling at ease. Some kids passing a ball back and forward. A boy with a dog. A girl with a cat. Two teenagers arm in arm, staring into each other's eyes. Somebody singing a sweet song somewhere. The long-haired busker with his guitar. Late birdsong. The sound of traffic. People everywhere, as if they were actors on a stage.

Stories everywhere.

Hand in hand, Antonia and Fleur walked through it all.

Fleur held Rosa close. "You'll be a star," she whispered.

She told herself that she could sense the vibrations of life in the brand-new puppet's body, sense the stirring of the brand-new puppet's mind.

37

Silvester and Puppet did sleep again.

Deep in the night, Silvester got up and went to find Puppet.

"How long will you last?" he asked him. "It can't be for ever."

No answer. Puppet lay dead still.

Silvester lifted him up carefully and carried him for the final time up the steep stairway to the attic.

The spiders dangled, the woodlice crawled, the owl hooted, the mouse squeaked.

At first, Silvester wasn't sure what to use. Then he found two mismatched half-made ancient arms and carved and sanded them into the shapes of wings. He removed Puppet's shirt and attached the wings to him, then covered them up again.

Then he carried Puppet back downstairs and laid him gently down to sleep.

"That makes me feel better," he said. "You'll be OK now, Puppet. Whatever happens, you'll be fine."

38

How do you make a stage? With bits and pieces, odds and ends, with hands and fingers, thoughts and dreams. That's how Fleur and Antonia made it. What would work as curtains? Curtains, of course. Antonia took a pair down from one of the unused rooms upstairs in the battered old cottage. Threadbare ancient dusty things, hanging from a rusty old curtain rod. They had the almost-lost patterns of unicorns on them.

But what would hold them up, and what would work as a frame for the stage? They had to be able to carry it all to the square and assemble it there. They tried sticks and broom handles. They tried fallen branches. They tried tying it all together with string and rope and tape, and they tried nailing bits together, but everything just turned out wonky and heavy and unwieldy, and every time they tried to stand something up it just fell down again. They talked of unscrewing the frame from one of the cottage doors and using that, and then they groaned and laughed at the daftness of the idea.

Then Antonia said, "Me. I'll be the frame."

"You, Mum?"

"Yes. I'll hold the curtain up high, then when the story's about to start, I'll pull it away. That's all we need, isn't it?

It's not like we're the Royal Opera House, is it?"

"No, it's not. So you'll be part of the stage, Mum?"

"Yes, I will. I'll *be* the stage!" She grinned. She stood up tall and held her arms out wide. "I'll make a very nice stage."

"You will!"

And for the platform? For the area the puppets would walk and dance upon? That was easy, they thought. They'd use the two old folding tables from the garden. They'd be simple enough to carry when they were folded up.

They pulled them together and tried it out. Yes, a very good firm platform.

Fleur stood Rosa upon it, but she had to reach her hands up high so that the puppet could dangle properly.

She frowned. "I need to be higher up."

"I have just the thing," her mum said.

She went into the cottage and came back with a little kitchen stool, and they put it behind the tables. Fleur stood on it. No need now to reach so high. She held Rosa's strings, and Rosa stood on the stage. Antonia tried the curtain trick, standing in front of the chairs and holding the curtains high and then sweeping the curtains aside and stepping aside herself. Fleur made Rosa bow as if an audience was there.

It was all manageable – the curtains, the tables, the stool. They'd be able to carry them easily to the square.

"We'll make some scenery, too," decided Fleur.

"Will we?"

176

"Yes. Simple backdrops. We'll paint them on sheets of paper. They'll show the world of the story."

"Yes," agreed her mum. "We'll paint a forest."

"And we'll paint the darkness in the forest."

"And the light that comes at the end."

"So much to do," said Fleur.

"Yes," said her mum. "So much that's wonderful to do."

And they kept on imagining, kept on creating.

"This is how it must have all started," said Antonia. "Wandering theatre groups going from place to place in long ago days, carrying the simple things they needed as they went along."

"Just like Silvester and Belinda did," said Fleur. "How beautiful."

"How very beautiful."

39

Sylvester & Fleur's MAGICAL Puppet Theatre

"That looks good, doesn't it, Rosa?" Fleur said. "Our names together. Silvester and Fleur. Just fancy that!"

She made the poster on the garden table. Rosa was propped up beside her. She drew pictures of Puppet and Rosa and coloured them in. Rosa's strings reached right up to the sky.

"There you are," she said to her puppet. "Recognize yourself?"

"*Yes,*" she made Rosa say.

"And there's your friend Kenneth. Don't you both look great?"

"*Yes!*" she made Rosa say again.

She drew the garden with its plants and trees and walls. She drew the horizontal oak tree branch with a pair of jackdaws on it. She made it look like a forest with darkness between the trees.

"See? It's just like a forest and just like a stage, isn't it, Rosa?"

She turned Rosa's head as if she was looking very closely at what Fleur had drawn.

"*Yes, it is,*" she made Rosa say. "*That's very clever.*"

"We'll take the garden and the forest to the square," said Fleur. "And you and Kenneth will be at the heart of the show."

"*That's lovely!*"

"Of course, there'll be a monster in it too."

179

"A monster?" Rosa's limbs rattled.

"Yes," said Fleur. "What good's a story without a monster in it?"

"What kind of monster?"

"A wolf or something. No, not a wolf. Wolves are lovely creatures. Something much, much more horrible than a wolf!"

Rosa rattled again. *"Will I be scared?"* she whispered.

"I expect so."

"Oh no!"

"But it'll turn out fine in the end. We'll be sure to keep each other safe. And you and Kenneth will be brave and bold."

"Will we?"

"You *are* a brave puppet, aren't you?"

Rosa seemed to ponder.

"Yes," Fleur made her whisper at last. *"Perhaps I am."*

But still Rosa rattled, and she seemed uncertain.

"Maybe I'll find out in the story if I am or if I'm not," she said. *"Maybe I'll find out when the monster comes."*

"Yes!" cried Fleur. "And maybe that's what the story's for."

Fleur held the cross-shaped piece of wood and walked Rosa through the garden. The clumsy puppets from a few days ago sat and lay upon the grass, and lounged against the walls, and dangled from the trees. The jackdaws and the other birds called from above. It was warm. Bees buzzed and butterflies danced. The scent of flowers was sweet.

Fleur got better at helping Rosa to move smoothly.

She tightened and adjusted. The strings didn't get entangled so easily. The arms and legs moved more elegantly.

Rosa's head turned from side to side as if she was admiring the garden.

They moved happily together through the shadows and the light.

"Jak! Jak!" called the jackdaws.

The pair moved over the curving pathways.

Then Fleur gasped and stopped. She set Rosa gently down among some primroses.

"Lie still," she said softly. "Be quiet. That might be the monster, just down there."

40

What was it? Nothing special. Just something bulging out of the soil. Something half buried, or maybe a dirty old root. Or was it stone? Fleur crouched down and touched it. Not stone. Wood. She scraped away some of the soil. She gripped it and tried to yank it out. It wouldn't budge. It must have been there for years. How far down did it go? She pushed away the soil around it and shoved and pulled it back and forward until it started to loosen. She stood up and kicked it, and forced it back and forward with her heel. Crouched down again and pulled again, but still it didn't want to come out.

"Come on," she whispered. It still looked like nothing special, but there was something about it. She kept on going. "Come *on*," she said again.

She gripped it with both hands. It came up a little. It was about as thick as her forearm. She rocked back on her heels and pulled and pulled. Something seemed to snap deep down, and here it came. She toppled backwards. It was lumpy and horrible, some sort of gnarled and ancient root. About as long as her forearm, too. She held it up. If you looked at it in the right way, it was a kind of monster. Three twisty legs. A scrawny tail of thin black shoots. A twisted lump for a head and snout with two more pointy shoots sticking up like horns. Two mismatched eyeholes.

Yes, a very good monster.

Fleur grinned. "Hello, you horror."

Insects were crawling on it and thin worms were slithering on it. She wiped more soil away. She held it closer. There was a rotten smell coming from it.

"You," she said, "are truly disgusting, mister."

There was some slimy stuff. She rubbed that away on the grass.

"You're much more disgusting and scary than any wolf could be!" She laughed. She held it out towards Rosa. "Look, Rosa," she said. "A proper monster!"

Rosa squeaked.

"It's called," said Fleur, "the Horror."

She got some string. She tied a length of it around the monster's thick and horrible neck and another length around one of its two horrible back legs. She moved the strings and the Horror lurched horribly across the grass.

She made it snarl and groan.

Rosa rattled.

"Just wait till Kenneth sees this," said Fleur. "He'll get the fright of his little life."

Then she picked Rosa up and laid the Horror down in her place. The monster looked ready to get up and start lumbering through the garden all on its own.

She glared at it. "Don't you dare," she said.

two

41

It's Saturday afternoon in this ordinary square in this ordinary town, so like so many other ordinary towns. People wandering about and chatting in the sunshine. Babies in buggies. Children walking, skipping, holding hands. A prowling cat or two. The sweet singing of birds in shrubs and on rooftops. Birds in flight. Pigeons dashing suddenly across the sky in a tight flock. The low drone of traffic. The thin vapour trail of a single plane high up in the blue, blue sky. The tops of distant hills far beyond the rooftops.

The cake shop is open, its window filled with brightly coloured cakes. Brightly clothed Laurence moves around inside. The butcher in his apron and cap glares out across his trays of meat. The door of Lisette's is open wide and Lisette inside sings sweetly as she works. Louis and his friends, along with others, sit at the cafe tables.

187

A poor drunken man leans against a low tree and stares glassily into the distance.

Near by, two lovers sit on a bench and gaze into each other's eyes. Another couple on another bench sit tense and grey-faced, sighing as they search for some answer to some problem known only to them.

The busker plays his guitar, head tilted. A girl sits close by, beating a little drum in rhythm with his tune.

Old people doze, babies gurgle, children play.

The town square. It's been here ever since this town began. It's ever changing. Marks of the past are everywhere. The old fountain where waster trickles from a spout in the ancient stone and back into the earth again. A stone horse trough, not used for years, now planted with brilliant flowers where bees buzz and butterflies dance. Faded writing on the shop walls, naming businesses long gone.

There's the stone memorial in the shape of a cross. It commemorates the many killed in old and cruel wars. A fading bunch of flowers lies below it.

It's a place, as it has always been, for people to wander, chat and play, to sit and wonder and dream, to feel excited, to feel forlorn, to feel lost and found. The air itself feels ancient. It's as if all of time is here. It seems as if every story that has ever occurred or has ever been created or has ever been told could exist right here.

It's a place that's perfect for a puppet play.

42

And here they are, at the far end of the square. Fleur and her mum. Our actors, our creators, carrying all they need to make a stage and a story.

Fleur has the rolled-up curtain and the rolled-up scenery across her shoulder. Rosa and the Horror dangle around her neck on their strings. She has the footstool in her hand. The folding tables are roped together and slung from Antonia's shoulder. They both carry little rucksacks. They're dressed in loose white trousers, loose white shirts. They move smoothly across the earth and through the light, at ease with each other, at ease in the world.

They come to the heart of the square. Antonia takes out a blanket that she spreads on the ground. They lay down their things and sit together. Beside them is a cherry tree. Fleur pins a poster to it.

Sylvester & Fleur's
MAGICAL
Puppet Theatre

The poster moves gently in the breeze.

It's early. Antonia lies back with her head resting on her hands and gazes into the blue and lets the warm sun shine down on her. Fleur sits forward, watching, listening. She waves at some children who run by.

Maddy Blenkinsop is in the square again. She puts on some spectacles, studies the poster.

"Now this looks interesting," she says. She smiles at Fleur. "I imagine you're Fleur."

Fleur laughs. "I am."

"Well done, dear."

Maddy ponders. "And Silvester?" she says. "Is he the one I might be thinking of?"

"I think he might be," says Fleur.

"Really? Well, I never."

She moves away.

Others come to look. Fleur informs them that whatever is to happen will happen a little later.

Time passes. No sign of Silvester or Puppet yet.

Antonia takes out some sandwiches and a flask of tea and they eat and drink.

More time passes. Still no Silvester.

Antonia lies back on the grass again and closes her eyes.

Has Silvester slept again? Will they have to go and wake him again, to bring him back to the world again?

Fleur again finds herself thinking that maybe this is all an illusion. Maybe Silvester and Kenneth have never been here at all. And she thinks that yes, Silvester was here, but this is how he intended it to be. He would show her how to make a puppet, and then he would disappear, and Fleur would become the puppet maker and the puppet master to take his place.

She shivers. She doesn't want that, not yet. She wants to create a show with Silvester, to see his puppet, Kenneth, and hers, Rosa, perform together on a makeshift stage, if only for a single time.

She looks towards the lane.

Nothing.

She eats and drinks. She talks to the folk who ask about the theatre. To some she says yes, it is the Silvester they remember. Yes, he is still working.

She thinks of her lost father. She knows he would be pleased to see her here with her mum, to see her holding Rosa and the Horror, to be preparing a show at the heart of their town.

She thinks of him with great sadness, but great joy as well.

She imagines her dad sitting there beside them on the grass.

She can almost feel him there.

She can almost hear his breath.

She holds Rosa close. She whispers to Rosa about her dad, how lovely he was, how funny, how kind, how she misses him so.

"It's how it will always be, I suppose," she whispers. "I'm happy, and I'll always be happy, and I'll always be sad as well. I'll always be dark and light." She sighs.

"You OK, my lovely?" murmurs her mum.

"Yes. I was thinking of Dad."

"Ah, me too."

"You too?"

"Yes. I was thinking how he would have loved to be with us today."

"He would, wouldn't he?"

"And he is with us in some way. In our hearts, in our minds, in our memories."

"Yes. He is."

Fleur looks into the empty air. "Hello, Dad," she whispers.

Antonia sits up and they hug each other. They wipe away tears, and they smile and smile.

Then there comes the single note of a distant trumpet, and here they are, Silvester and Puppet, emerging from the almost-forgotten lane, entering the square.

"There he is at last!" says Fleur.

193

43

Silvester and Puppet walk into the square hand in hand. Puppet is jerky as ever, quick as ever. They pause for a moment by their friends at the cafe table. Silvester waves to acknowledge calls from passers-by.

They approach the middle of the square. Puppet gives a little skip and quickens his step as he sees his waiting friends. Silvester lets go of his hand and Puppet runs in excitement, calling out, "Jam! Jam! Jam!"

Fleur and her mum see that Silvester has a battered silver trumpet hanging around his neck. He grins as he draws closer. He lifts the trumpet to his lips and toots again.

"Found it!" he exclaims. "One of the few things that didn't go off to the museum."

He toots again. People stop and look.

Silvester grins. "Not yet," he says. "Not yet!"

"Good afternoon, Silvester," says Antonia.

"Good afternoon, everyone," replies Silvester.

He sees the poster on the tree. He says that it is beautiful.

"And look," says Fleur, showing him the materials they have brought with them. "Everything we need to make our stage."

He laughs. "You truly are just like we were!"

He looks towards the sky.

"Do you see, Belinda?" he says softly. "They truly are just like we were!"

And he breathes deeply and spreads his arms wide in joy.

"What a splendid day is this!" he says. "On such a day as this, anything at all seems possible."

"Would you like a sandwich?" asks Fleur's mum. She holds one towards him. "This one is Cheddar cheese and pickle."

"Antonia, you must have known. How can I resist?"

He sits with them. Fleur unrolls the scenery.

"A forest," she explains. "And a very dark forest at that. A forest filled with dappled light. Just what we need!"

Silvester smiles. "It's all that is ever needed."

He drinks some tea.

"Silvester," says Fleur. "Will you be the monster?"

"The monster?"

"Yes, all tales need a monster, don't they?"

"They do indeed. How else can the goodness in a story shine so bright?"

She shows him the monster she created from the thing that she yanked out of the earth.

"It is called the Horror," she says.

He widens his eyes. He recoils. He takes it from her hands.

"What a splendid monster!" he cries. He holds it out towards Puppet. "Have you ever seen anything like that, Puppet?"

Puppet stares. "Jam!" he says. He holds Claude out before his face as if to fend the Horror off.

Silvester laughs. He holds the Horror before his own face and glares at it.

"Yes," he says. "It will be an honour to play this part."

They begin to assemble the stage.

They unfold the two tables and place them edge to edge. They place the stool behind them. Fleur's mum demonstrates how she will work the curtains. She shows them how she will hold the scenery as the puppets act. The scenery is rolled up between sticks, like scrolls.

She laughs as she kneels and holds the scenery above the stage.

"It's all a bit shambolic," she admits.

"Yes," says Silvester. "Shambolic and beautiful, and tentative and brave. This is how everything begins and how everything began."

He smiles tenderly. "You're wonderful, Antonia," he says. "Each one of us is wonderful."

He gives a sudden blast on the trumpet.

"Let's call them in," he says.

He gives another blast.

"That'll wake them all up!"

44

And it does wake them up. Many people stop and stare, head in their direction. Already several people are sitting and waiting on the grass. Children in little groups. Families. Silvester toots again. Birds flutter away and flutter back again. Teenagers loiter. Some old folk whisper, point at Silvester, whisper again.

"Welcome, my friends!" Silvester calls. "Welcome to Fleur and Silvester's Magical Puppet Theatre. We are rather small – but we are strong. We are shambolic – but we are brave. Come closer. Yes, closer. Don't be scared. Don't be shy. Come close. Be bold. Allow us to bend your minds and move your hearts and touch your souls today."

Silvester seems so tall and strong. How wonderful to be before an audience again. How happy he is to be with his puppets and his friends in this square at the heart of his town.

As he calls, the people gather. They stroll across the pavements and the grass. There are the two boys who fought about the bedroom ghost. There are the teenagers in love. And the big boys who bullied Puppet and who said sorry. Across the square, Laurence watches and waves from the door of Cakes of Heaven.

"Let me introduce our actors!" Silvester calls.

He lifts Puppet onto the stage.

"This is Puppet, of whom I am very proud! His name is also Kenneth. Take a bow, Kenneth."

He gently presses Puppet's shoulders, and as if he understands, Puppet leans forward in a bow.

"Have you anything to say to our audience before we begin?" asks Silvester.

"Jam!" says Puppet. "Jam!"

Children laugh. "Jam!" they call back at him. "Jam!"

Puppet laughs straight back again. His limbs and body rattle in excitement.

"And here," says Silvester, "is his dear friend Rosa. She is a little younger than Kenneth, but of course no less wonderful, no less astonishing. Come forward, little Rosa."

Fleur, standing on the stool, guides Rosa with the cross-shaped piece of wood. She is still learning, still a little uncertain, and Rosa moves awkwardly. But Fleur guides her so that she stands right by Puppet at the centre of the stage. Fleur dips the wood forward and Rosa dips her head and bows.

"What would you like to say, dear Rosa?" asks Silvester.

"Hello, everyone," Fleur makes Rosa say in a sweet shy voice. *"It is lovely to be with you all today."*

And the audience applaud, already entranced, already falling in love with those who will perform for them today.

Puppet takes out Claude. He holds him out to the audience and flies him through the air.

"Oh, and little Claude, of course!" says Silvester. "How could I forget the smallest and yet the oldest of our cast?"

There are cries to say how sweet Claude is, how delicate and small, how lovely all these actors are.

Silvester raises a finger in warning.

"I must tell you that we have another," he says, "who must remain hidden and unknown for now. Perhaps those who are fearful should step away now and return to gentler pursuits – swinging on swings or playing with cats or eating ice cream."

He pauses. He stares into the eyes of the audience.

"The puppet theatre," he says ominously, "can be a dark and dangerous and scary place. So yes, perhaps those who are frail, or perhaps those who are simply rather young, will wish to step away."

He leans towards a little family on the grass close by him. Two adults, and a little boy, a little girl.

"You, for instance," he says. "Do you wish to leave before we start? Are you scared of being scared?"

The children are wide-eyed. They snuggle closer to each other and to the adults. They giggle.

"No!" they cry, eyes burning with excitement and trepidation.

No one moves away. Many move closer.

Silvester smiles and spreads his arms wide.

"So, you are all still here?" he says. "Brave souls, each and every one of you."

Indeed, they are all still here. And they settle. They watch. They wait. They watch these people standing before them, preparing to perform for them.

"Then so be it," Silvester says. "And now, ladies and gentlemen, boys and girls, cats and dogs, you must also do your preparations, just as we do."

He leans forward. He stares, hypnotic.

"Empty your minds," he says softly. "Forget the world. Forget your plans. Forget your troubles. Forget *yourselves*. Relax and look into this stage, this space. I give you Fleur and Silvester's Magical Puppet Theatre!"

45

Now Antonia stands before the stage. She holds up the curtain high on its pole, and the stage and the actors are hidden. She waits a few moments, then draws the curtain away, and the stage is exposed again. There are Puppet and Rosa, waiting to begin. There is Fleur on her stool, holding Rosa's strings. There is Silvester, the director, the narrator, at the side of the stage.

Antonia then moves to the back of the stage. She kneels down by Fleur and holds up the first scroll. It is a simple picture, drawn with pencils and paint and ink. It shows a forest in the daytime. Many trees, dense foliage, branches twisting up into the sky. There are deer, a fox, birds on the boughs and in the sky. A blue sky, a yellow sun.

Puppet and Rosa stand before the forest, and within it.

"We bring you a simple tale," Silvester begins. "A very familiar tale. Two children decide one day to wander together into the forest close by their home. Are they old enough? Are they brave enough? Of course they are! Their parents know they are. And they know this forest. It is near by. It is so familiar. It is so beautiful. The children say goodbye to their parents."

"*Bye-bye,*" says Rosa.

"Jam," says Puppet.

"And of course," says Silvester, "the parents say, *Goodbye, dear children. Don't go too far, and don't get lost.*"

And Antonia speaks, from behind her scroll.

"*And don't be late coming home. Be back by dark. Remember!*"

"*Of course, Mummy and Daddy,*" Fleur makes Rosa say. "*Do not be concerned. Bye-bye. Bye-bye.*"

"Jam," says Puppet. "Jam."

Puppet now takes Rosa's hand, just as Silvester took Puppet's hand when they stepped together into the world for the very first time. He leans towards Rosa, as if to tell her, *Don't be nervous. I will take care of you. I will be with you always.*

"And so," says Silvester, "into the forest they go."

The puppets' feet move, click-clack, click-clack. They move nowhere, just a few inches back and forth of this just-created

203

stage before this just-created scenery. And yet, as the audience relax, as people forget themselves and allow themselves to care for Puppet and Rosa and Claude, they are drawn into the tale. They look with the wide-open eyes of the imagination, and it really does seem that there might truly be a vast forest, in that little space in this town square. There are the deer slipping through the trees. There are the shining eyes of the fox. There are the birds flying. There are the sounds of little feet as the children walk, walk deeper into the forest.

For those who allow themselves to believe it, who allow themselves to see, it really does seem that Puppet and Rosa take track after track after track.

"Deeper, deeper in they go," says Silvester. "The forest is so beautiful. See the light shining down through the trees. Look, see the deer and the fox. See how Kenneth and Rosa stay close together. They're not scared. See how happy they are. See how merry they are in their wandering. What a wonderful hour they spend together in the woods. And on they go, hand in hand, their little feet going tap-tap-tap."

He pauses. The puppets move. The forest deepens in the imaginations of the audience.

Silvester waits. And then music starts. It is the long-haired busker with his guitar. He too has been drawn here. He strums a simple tune with simple walking rhythms. And a girl with a drum is with him. She softly beats it. Silvester smiles. Music enhances the tale as it always does. Music charms and entrances.

"And time passes," says Silvester after some moments, "as it always does. Light changes, as it always does. Oh, now darkness is coming on. And the children become afraid. They begin to shudder."

And they do. Fleur rattles Rosa fast. The guitarist and the drummer quicken their rhythms, darken their notes.

Rosa cries, *"Oh no, the darkness! We must go back, Kenneth!"*

And then the scene is changed. Down comes the scenery of the daytime forest, and here is the scroll of the forest at night. Most of it is deep jet black. There is a crescent moon aglow in the sky. The trees – their trunks, their branches, their foliage – are etched in white as if picked out by the moon. There is a pale owl, and another.

Behind the white etchings there is darkness, darkness, darkness.

The guitar plays. The drum beats.

"Oh, Kenneth!" cries Rosa. *"What shall we do?"*

"Jam!"

"Oh, Kenneth, how shall we ever find our way home?"

"Jam!"

"Oh, Kenneth, who is there to protect us?"

"The poor children," says Silvester. "They have lost their way. They are so forlorn and so exposed and all alone. They wonder why they ever entered the forest. And they are so tired. The need for sleep threatens to overwhelm them. So they lie down in a clearing lit by the moon."

Fleur lets Rosa crumple to the earth. Puppet follows her. And they lie together, there on the stage.

"Maybe all will be well," says Silvester. "Maybe they will sleep, and wake, and find their way back home again in the morning."

But then the stage itself begins to shudder. The whole earth seems to shudder. The music of the guitar is twisted into a harsh noise. And there comes a deep growling, a grunting, a vicious snarling. And oh, the Horror rises from the earth! It is an ugly lumpy stinky thing dangling on string from Silvester's hands.

"Kenneth! Kenneth!" cries Rosa. *"Look! It is the Horror!"*

Silvester himself turns ugly now. He makes the grunts. He makes the snarls. He makes the Horror slither closer, closer. The children in the audience recoil. They are petrified. It seems they cannot move. They whimper.

But just as the Horror seems about to strike, brave Puppet suddenly finds his courage. He stands up to the horrid thing. He raises his hands and calls out, *"Jak! Jak!* Jam! Jam!"

The Horror keeps on slithering, snarling, grunting. What is this little puppet to a horror such as he?

But this is Kenneth, our bold brave Puppet. He rushes at the Horror and he kicks it with his hard little foot. He raises his arms high and makes himself appear to be immense, and he kicks again, again. The Horror is astonished. It growls and snarls again. But the stupid cruel Horror is no match for angry Kenneth defending himself, defending Rosa and Claude, defending the goodness in the world.

And oh, that Horror! What a coward it turns out to be. Perhaps it imagined that children lost in the forest must be frail and timid things. Perhaps it imagined that all children must bow down before it and be turned to quivering little wrecks. Not our Kenneth. Not our Rosa. Not the brave young people of the world today.

Kick, goes Kenneth. *Kick-kick,* "Jam!"

And see how the Horror backs away, how it slithers back into the earth from which it came.

And people cheer and laugh and applaud. Children's eyes shine with delight.

"Well done, Kenneth!" they call. "You're a hero, Kenneth!"

Silvester raises his hands.

There's a moment of stillness and calm as Kenneth stares into the space where the Horror had been, as if to check that it has really gone.

Silvester widens his eyes as he looks at the audience.

"Yes," he says. "I think it's gone."

Then Rosa lies down and Puppet copies her.

And the music and the drumbeat soften again.

"Now that the Horror has been defeated," says Silvester, "Kenneth and Rosa lie down again in the clearing. They know that the light will return and they will be home again tomorrow. So they fall to sleep. And the forest once more comes to life around them. The world turns and dawn arrives."

New scenery rises. The dark forest is gone. Now there is a forest filled with the golden light of dawn. There are bright flowers. There are birds, deer, a fox.

Puppet and Rosa sit up. They shake away the dreams and nightmares from their minds.

"And now," Silvester says, "they hear voices calling."

"*Children!*" comes a cry from Antonia.

"*Mummy! Daddy!*" calls out Rosa.

And Rosa and Kenneth stand up, and rattle as they move, rattle as their feet move faster, faster, drawn to the voices calling them back home again, drawn to their dear parents come to find them once again.

And now Fleur picks up Rosa and holds her to her chest, and Silvester picks up Puppet and holds him to his chest. And Antonia takes Claude and holds him to her chest. And they are all together again, puppets and puppet makers, children and parents.

They turn to face the audience and they smile and bow.

"So it is done," says Silvester. "All is well. The children have done what children do in tales such as this. They face the darkness, and they triumph and survive."

They all bow again. The audience applaud again.

The guitar player strums his final simple notes.

And a boy's voice calls out, "Again! Again!" It is Tom, the boy from the swings park. He is with his mother.

"Again?" asks Silvester.

"Yes!" says Tom.

His mother leans down to whisper in his ear.

"Yes," he says. "Again. *Please*."

And others take up the call.

"Again! Again!"

Silvester smiles. He turns to Fleur and her mother. They smile.

"Yes," he says. "In just a little while."

46

"Well, what did you think?" asks Silvester.

"It was *great*!" says Antonia.

They're sitting together behind the stage. Laurence appears with a trayful of cakes. He bows and lays it on the grass beside them.

He grins. "I have of course included the essential jam tart."

He waves away the banknote that Silvester offers him.

"No," he says. "It is a great honour. And now I will leave you to relax, as I have been told that you will do another show before the day is done."

And off he goes.

They eat.

"It was rather *short*," says Fleur.

"Short?" says Silvester.

"Yes. It all flew by. Maybe we need to put more into the story to make it a bit longer and more interesting."

"Such as?"

"Well, they could... They could meet someone else, for instance, not just the Horror."

"Like who?"

"Like a ... like a talking deer!"

"A talking deer?"

"Yes. Or a *singing* deer! It sings, sings of the forest to them."

She starts la-la-la-la-ing like a singing deer and bursts out laughing at herself. How weird it is that these ideas just jump into her mind, like they were already in there, or like they've flown like little birds into her brain! She stops singing suddenly.

"Or a talking wolf!" she says. "But not a scary wolf. We've got enough scariness with that horrible Horror, haven't we? Maybe a wolf that complains that people always say wolves are scary when they're not."

"That's a nice idea," says Silvester. He laughs as well, at the way ideas burst into life.

"And maybe the wolf gives Kenneth a ride on his back," says Fleur. "That'd be great!"

"And Rosa too?"

"Yes! She will be scared at first, of course. She is a rather nervous girl. But once she gets over that she'll love it. She'll love the wolf and so will Kenneth."

Fleur gasps as the ideas rush through her.

"And the wolf could come to help them defeat the Horror. Or no, maybe not. Maybe that really has to be Kenneth's job. But it could carry them home again on its back! Imagine it dashing through the forest in the dawn. And it could—"

"One problem," says Silvester.

"What's that?"

"We haven't got a wolf puppet. Nor a deer either, now I come to think of it."

211

"We'll make them for next time!"

Silvester laughs. "You really are like we were. Soon you'll have a house full of puppets and a head spinning with stories."

"In the meantime," says Fleur, "we can have an imaginary singing deer and an imaginary talking wolf. If we tell people that they're there, they'll at least be able to see them in their mind's eye, won't they?"

"Yes. They will. They will see the most beautiful deer and the most powerful and gorgeous wolf. I'll include them in the next show when I'm telling the tale."

"Brilliant."

Fleur nibbles a piece of chocolate cake.

"And it *is* rather small," she says.

"Small?"

"Yes. There's not really space to move around much, is there? Especially if we're going to move on to having talking deer and a wolf running about with puppets on its back."

"So we need a bigger stage?"

"Yes. This is fine for now, but we need to start *thinking* of a bigger stage."

They all look at the stage. In their mind's eye, they see it bigger, grander, a bigger space with an arch and curtains and a wider platform. And for a moment, Silvester wonders if he was wrong to give so much away to the museum. There were stages and puppets aplenty. He could have passed them all on to Fleur. But the thought passes. No, it has to begin afresh. It all has to be recreated. It all has to have a brand-new life.

"In the end," he says, "we had many stages of many sizes. Tiny ones that we took into nurseries and schools. Bigger ones that we erected in parks. One year, a massive one that was created for us at a puppet festival in Tuscany. And of course many, many puppets of many, many sizes and many, many kinds."

Fleur's eyes glow as she imagines such wonders.

"It must have been amazing," she says.

"It was. We grew story by story, show by show, stage by stage. We got bigger and better, but we stayed shambolic and imperfect at the heart. That is how the puppet world must be. Never perfect. Always a bit rittly-rattly. Always changing, always growing. And the stories will keep on coming and coming and growing and growing, like there can never be an end to them, which of course there can't."

47

Word is getting out about the show. Sol and Francis appear. They say they're so happy to see Silvester at work again. They say that the display at the museum is developing very well.

Francis laughs. "You will be remembered for evermore!" he says.

Louisa, the woman writing the book about Silvester's world, turns up too.

"It did seem impossible, Silvester, to think of you giving up," she says.

"Giving up," he says. "It seems I need to keep on *starting* up."

Louisa crouches down and stares at Puppet, then stares at Silvester.

"So many things seem impossible," she says. "And then they seem to become possible after all."

She frowns. She takes a breath and seems about to say something, but she says nothing, just stares at Silvester again, then finally whispers, "He's wonderful, Silvester."

Silvester shrugs. "His name is Kenneth," he says. "He's a good lad."

He calls Puppet's name and Puppet turns.

"This is Louisa," he tells him. "She's writing a book about me. Maybe one day she'll write a book about you."

"Jam!" says Puppet.

Silvester laughs. "That would be a very good title," he agrees.

Children come to look at the stage and the puppets. Kenneth holds out Claude to them. Like Louisa, they stare at Puppet, but they say nothing except that he is lovely, that he is brilliant. He does a little dance for them and his limbs click and clack and they say, "Jam! Jam!"

Fleur makes Rosa talk and sing for them and they are

distracted. She shows them how to pick up sticks and turn them into puppets just by looking at them in a particular way and moving them in a particular way. Soon children are stepping weirdly shaped sticks across the grass. They're giving the sticks names and speaking through them in sticky puppety voices.

Close by, the busker and the drummer keep on playing.

Children ask when the next show will begin, and Fleur and Silvester look at each other and say soon, very soon.

Silvester gazes into the sky.

"A little later, perhaps," he says, "when there's more darkness in the world."

He sighs and yawns. He lies down on the grass and stares up into the ever-changing sky.

"Are you OK, Silvester?" asks Antonia.

"I am very happy," he says. "I am very pleased by all of this. But I'm very tired."

He closes his eyes. He seems to sleep.

Puppet goes to him and lies with his head in Silvester's lap and seems to be sleeping too.

Time passes in the square, as it does everywhere. Day turns to afternoon, which begins to turn to dusk. The sun falls towards the hills beyond the rooftops. The single street light at the centre of the square comes on, and lights up the air, lights up the earth and the little stage below.

"When," asks a little boy, "will there really *be* another show?"

Gently Antonia touches Silvester's brow.

He opens his eyes.

"Now?" he says. "Is it time?"

"Yes, if you're ready."

He smiles, sighs, stands up.

He takes Puppet's hand and helps him to his feet.

"I'm ready," he softly says.

48

And so, as daylight fades and the streetlight shines more brightly, they create the final show. Silvester tells the tale. His enchanting voice charms the listeners. His rhythms lead them to the edge of dreams. The busker and the drummer accompany him.

The puppets begin their click-clack walk. They enter the forest, hand in hand. Very soon they come across the deer, and the deer sings to them about the beauty of the forest, its dappled light, its beasts and birds, its flowers and ferns, its ancientness. It leaps away, for it must tend to its fawns, and the children walk on. On unknown tracks, through sunlit clearings, past huge oaks and beech trees. They step over woodland flowers and across trickling streams and shallow pools.

Time passes, and they walk in growing trepidation, for

they know that they are becoming lost. Darkness falls and the Horror rises, and brave Kenneth overcomes it, as he always will whenever this tale is told. They lie down to rest in a moonlit clearing. And now Silvester tells of the wolf. It approaches at the first frail signs of dawn. It is a great muscular and handsome creature filled with strength and kindness. The children awake to find it there beside them.

"Do not be troubled," it says to them. *"I'm pleased that I have found you."*

The wolf allows the children on his back and they feel the great power of him. This is the wolf which carries them out of the forest and back home again. And many in the audience do see the deer and the wolf in their minds, almost as clearly as they see Kenneth and Rosa, almost as if they are truly there on the stage.

And there are others here too, as the tale is told. They step out from memory and dreams and imagination. As Fleur moves Rosa on her strings, she looks up and sees her father there, at the very edge of the light. They gaze at each other, and they smile, and then he is gone. And as Silvester moves word by word, image by image, scene by scene, through the story, he too looks up and he sees others there, among the audience at the edge of light. He sees his lovely Belinda. He sees puppets from the past. He sees his own mother, smiling at him as she did so long ago when he was just a little boy.

He keeps on telling the tale, telling the tale, holding

everyone together, until once more the tale is done and the children are safely home again.

And when it is done, they all bow, Silvester, Fleur, Puppet, Rosa, Antonia.

There is much applause that echoes across the square and spreads out into the town.

Many say it is so good to see Silvester at work again.

He holds out his hands towards Fleur.

"She will carry it on," he says. "Nothing has ended. It all starts again."

☆ ☆ ☆

Silvester, Fleur and Antonia take down the stage and fold everything away. They eat the last of the cakes together.

Many come with thanks, admiration, congratulations.

"It was a good show," says Silvester. "But as always we'll work to make it better."

"Yes, a good show!" agrees Fleur. "And the best day of my life!"

They're all so tired. They hug each other and part and say they will see each other again soon.

Silvester has a glass of wine with Louis and his wife at a table with a hooded candle burning. Puppet stands at his side and waits.

Silvester says it has been a long day. He says he has rarely been happier. He turns and looks back into the square at the

221

heart of his town. Some children play beneath the streetlight. A cat moves through the shadows. The busker gently plays. In the distance are the silhouettes of Antonia and Fleur, walking away, carrying the puppet theatre, heading back home.

Silvester leaves his friends and heads with Puppet back into the almost-forgotten lane and back home again.

They lie down to sleep. Silvester holds Puppet against his chest and night passes by.

At first light, Puppet nudges Silvester, but he doesn't wake.

"Jam," he whispers. "Jam."

He touches Silvester's brow with his three-fingered hand.

"Dad. Dad."

He kicks the bed. *Kick-kick whack-whack kick-kick.*

Silvester doesn't stir.

Puppet kicks again.

He whispers, *"Jam"* and *"Jak."*

Silvester doesn't wake.

"Dad," Puppet whispers. "Da-ad."

He kicks again. But it's halfhearted.

Puppet knows.

And if Puppet had tears that could fall, they would be fall-ing now.

Puppet gets up and stands in the silent house. He tucks Claude into his pocket, opens the front door and leaves. He walks through the lane into the square. Early morning. No one has risen yet. Everything is silent, except for the click and clack

222

of his hard little feet, the rattle of his mismatched limbs, the chorus of the birds.

All alone, he makes his way through the streets to Fleur and Antonia's house.

He comes to the gate and kicks at it.

He kicks again, again.

After a time, Fleur is there at the other side.

"Who's there?" she asks.

"Jam, jam."

Fleur hauls the gate open. Her mum is behind her now.

They see dear Kenneth.

He stands very silent and very still.

He gazes at them through his bright green eyes.

And they know what Puppet knows.

49

What can a puppet do without his puppet maker? How can he truly live? What can possibly come next?

With Fleur and Antonia, Puppet attended the celebrations of Silvester's wonderful life. He lived with them for some time in their cottage.

But the life that had been given to Puppet in the attic in the middle of one extraordinary night was beginning to drain from him. He stumbled more often. He had long periods when he seemed not to be here at all, when there was no movement in him, when he seemed to be just a collection of odds and ends, of mismatched bits and pieces, a thing of wood and string and paint and nothing more. It seemed he might simply fall apart, which is the destiny of so many puppets.

At times like that, Fleur and her mum left him to sit on the grass and lie back against a tree, or to rest in a garden chair.

Fleur, meanwhile, was filled with energy. The spirit of Silvester was within her. She made puppets and props and painted scenery for the shows that she would go on to create. She wrote plays and stories and songs and dreamed of travelling the country and the world with her own puppet theatre. That would surely come to pass.

Sometimes Puppet would rise, and say his simple words,

and call up to the jackdaws and the finches, and gaze through his bright green eyes into the bright blue sky. And sometimes Fleur brought Rosa to him, and they wandered happily through the garden together as they used to do.

But they all knew that the story of Puppet soon would be done.

Late one afternoon, Fleur was at the garden table, smoothing the features of a puppet called Elaine. Puppet lay with his back against one of the ancient massive oak trees. He had been there unmoving since early morning.

Fleur looked up when she saw Puppet rising.

He turned his face towards her for a moment. He held up his hand in a kind of greeting.

The tree above him was filled with singing birds.

She wanted to go to him but she dared not move. She just watched as he took off his shirt and laid it on the grass.

There were the makeshift wings.

Puppet took Claude from his pocket and seemed to whisper to him. He held up his hand to Fleur again.

All she could say was, "Oh, Kenneth."

And then he rose from the grass and through the branches of the great oak into the sky.

Fleur stood up now. She called her mother. Together they saw Puppet move over the garden wall and the rooftops towards the setting sun. All around him, the birds were singing. Perhaps others saw him and thought little of it. It was a jackdaw, a crow, a pigeon heading back to roost before the night came on.

Fleur and Antonia stood on tiptoe.

They stared and stared as Puppet turned into a distant dot against the orange sun and then into nothing at all.

Nobody knows where he went. Perhaps to a place of many, many puppets. Perhaps he is with Silvester and Belinda, in some distant unknown place where they make stories and perform shows together, where they take tracks through dappled forests and defeat the monsters and meet talking deer and kindly wolves, and help lost children to find their way home again, where they walk hand in hand together through the shadows and the light, and Kenneth the puppet's limbs click-clack as he walks, as he skips and says, "Jak jak, jam jam, Dad, Mam."

David Almond is the acclaimed author of *Skellig*, *My Name Is Mina*, *Brand New Boy*, *The Dam*, *A Way to the Stars* and many more novels, stories, picture books, plays and opera librettos, and his work is published in numerous languages. His major awards include the Carnegie Medal and the Hans Christian Andersen Award, the world's most prestigious prize for children's authors. In 2021 he was awarded an OBE for services to literature. David lives on the north-east coast of England.

Lizzy Stewart has written and illustrated books for both adults and children, and her picture book *There's a Tiger in the Garden* won both the Waterstones Children's Book Prize and a World Illustration Award. She teaches illustration at Goldsmiths, University of London and has also taught courses at the Tate and on behalf of the National Portrait Gallery. Lizzy lives in London.